Wish Riders

PATRICK JENNINGS

HYPERION BOOKS FOR CHILDREN

New York

To Jean T.,
of whom I am overly fond

Printed in the United States of America
First Edition
1 3 5 7 9 10 8 6 4 2
Library of Congress Cataloging-in-Publication Data on file.
Reinforced binding
ISBN 1-4231-0010-7

Visit www.hyperionbooksforchildren.com

"For there is hope of a tree, if it be cut down, that it will sprout again, and that the tender branch thereof will not cease."
—Job 14:7

CHAPTER
One

Edith knew gulls, knew this one was about to scream, covered her ears. It screamed twice, chuckled, hopped down from the windowsill to the dresser, talons scrabbling on the lacquered wood. Its head swiveled, tilted; its unblinking eyes fell upon her sitting on her bunk, her knees tucked under her chin, arms wrapped round her folded legs. She was sure it was the same bird, the one that had lit on the hazel branch in her backyard at home, the branch Edith had planted for her mother. Gulls never came so deep into the woods.

The bird trod on her hairbrush, stabbed at the bristles with its beak, pulled loose a snarl of wiry, sandy hair, held it up. Building a nest? Edith wondered. The gull fluttered back to the sill, its whiteness glowing against the drabness of the camp outside. It unfolded its wings, flapped, flew off, Edith's hair in its bill. Edith jumped down from the bed, ran to the window, craned her head out. Rain mizzled her face. As before when the bird had flown, Edith felt a chill in her bones.

"There you are!" a voice shrieked behind her, a voice like the gull's, the voice of Hero, Edith's "sister." "Mother Smith's lookin' for you an' she's mad as a hornet. I'd get myself to the cookhouse if I was you. Thank the Lord I ain't."

Hero's face was unfairly fine: dainty nose, delicate chin, rosy cheeks, bee-stung lips, eyes the color of robins' eggs, creamy skin despite the rigors of camp life. Right then this lovely face was twisted in spite, mocking the golden ringlets that framed it. Hero was sixteen, Edith's elder by a year. She always spoke to Edith in this manner, though Edith had never done a thing to her. Hero had spent the bulk of her life at Camp Nine, had worked for Mother and Father Smith for more than a decade, which was enough, Edith thought, to embitter anyone. Edith had been in camp only a month, but could already feel herself souring.

"I'll be along," she said.

"You're gettin' the switch, y'know," Hero said, her eyes glinting. "An' the longer it takes you to meet it, the more lashes you'll get." She turned, pranced off.

Edith smoothed the blanket on her bunk, tugged the hairbrush through her flypaper hair, thought of the gull, hustled through the morning drizzle toward the cookhouse.

Like most of the other buildings in Camp Nine— the bunkhouses, bathhouses, equipment sheds, pool hall, camp office, camp store—the cookhouse was the size and shape of a railroad car, less the wheels. This made it easy to hoist the camp onto flatcars when time came to move on to a new show; that is, whenever an area's harvestable timber had been depleted. The cookhouse abutted the mess hall, which was three cars laid end to end with doorways cut between them.

Edith stopped at the door, took a few deep breaths, composed herself, opened the door, strode with her shoulders back, chin up, ready to look Mother Smith dead in the eye, dare her to complain. The woman silently conveyed her displeasure with a razor-sharp glance. Edith cloaked her relief with indifference. She knew the only reason Mother Smith didn't fetch a switch was that she was simply too busy at that moment to whip anyone.

Hero's pretty face, dusted with flour, registered her disappointment. Edith gave her a wink. Hero squinted at her. Edith was sure Hero needed eyeglasses, figured the Smiths were too tightfisted to spring for them.

Edith collected a cart of warm dishes and wheeled it to the farthest car of the mess hall, which, like the others, held six picnic tables in two rows with a narrow aisle between. She began laying out towers of crockery: plate, overturned bowl, saucer, overturned coffee cup. She worked her way down the tables like a machine—plate-bowl-saucer-cup, plate-bowl-saucer-cup—stopping now and then to drop tin utensils into one of the two coffee cans placed in the center of each table. Setting was the chore Edith most enjoyed, it being clean, solitary, and mathematical. She calculated her progress: twenty settings, one fifth done; twenty-five, a quarter; fifty, a half. . . . She liked the musical sound of the stacking (*tunk*, *tink*, *tunk*), imagined the crash of the utensils as percussion. She had often gone to the symphony with her mother, back when . . . She shook the memory away.

Tunk, tink, tunk, crash; tunk, tink, tunk, crash.

Edith started losing her grip around setting number eighty, due more to giddiness than fatigue. She rarely reached ninety before her movements started seeming comical, ridiculous, like something out of a Charlie Chaplin picture. After all, she was not a machine. Acknowledging this was the beginning of the end. The wisest thing would be for her to relinquish the task, let someone else—Hero, or her other "sister," Perdie—complete the job, but she never did, never would. Giddiness at Camp Nine was too precious.

A cup upended a saucer at place setting eighty-six.

The saucer shattered on the plank bench, the pieces tinkling onto the plank floor.

"For the love of Christ!" Mother Smith screamed from the kitchen.

"Sorry!" Edith called back, quickly gathering up the shards in her apron, dumping them into a tub on the cart.

She completed the final seventeen settings. A hundred and three bachelor loggers lived in camp—twice as many as had a month prior—but an even hundred served Edith's computations better. She pushed the empty cart back to the kitchen.

"Ever' time," whispered Perdie. "She should put me on settin'. Jes' look at my hands." She showed Edith how red and chapped they were.

Like Edith, Perdie was lanky as lumber—or, as their nine-year-old "brother," Mickey, put it—flat as boards. Perdie had a crookedness about her, as if her legs were odd lengths, her shoulders uneven, her arms out of joint. The loggers said she had a hitch in her get-along. Her nails and bottom lip were ragged from constant gnawing. Her hair, which was black as pitch, hung straight and limp; so black, straight, and limp that rumor had it she was Indian. Her brown skin did nothing to dispel the rumors.

"You'd break less?" Edith replied, grinning.

Perdie snorted her horsey laugh. "More, I bet."

"Edith," grunted Mrs. Keckonius, the cook. "Cut this into biscuits for me."

"Yes, ma'am," Edith answered, scurrying over.

By her own reckoning, as well as by the men's, Mrs. Keckonius was the best hasher on the peninsula, making her the camp's most valuable asset. Good food kept loggers from skipping off. They'd put up with hard bunks, drafty privies, cold water, bedbugs, lice, but not bad grub. The Smiths ran the camp; Jacobs & Williams owned it—but Mrs. Keckonius fueled the men that made it work. Her orders were obeyed promptly and to the letter. Mother Smith tolerated nothing less.

With the open end of a tin can, Edith punched circles out of a swath of floured dough, tossed them onto a greased baking sheet.

"After that, start on the lunch buckets," Mrs.

Keckonius said, not looking up from her smoking griddle, where sausages, bacon, and eggs sizzled, a pot of oatmeal stewed. Mrs. Keckonius went down the rows of flapjacks, turning them with a seasoned flick of the wrist. She was a sturdy woman, over six feet tall, shoulders broad, jaw square as any logger's. She was fifty-six years old, daughter of Finnish immigrants, mother of two, grandmother of five, and, as she often remarked, wife to no man. "The 'Mrs.' is to scare off busybodies and scoundrels," she said. She was as strong and sure a person, man or woman, as Edith had ever met. For this reason Edith did as Mrs. Keckonius bade without resentment.

The loggers began filing in as Edith was loading the last of their lunch buckets. They did so in a somber, orderly fashion, a hundred-plus giants spitting out snoose into a tin bucket, hanging a hundred-plus coats and hats on a hundred-plus pegs. The smell of breakfast was overwhelmed by the heady smells of tobacco, boot grease, pipe smoke, kerosene, clothes that had been labored in for days. The men wore tin pants with suspenders (never overalls; overalls were strictly for hoosiers, that is, for farmers; farming was as low a calling a man could have, according to the loggers), calked boots, sweat-stained newsboy caps or fedoras, a wide variety of bandages and splints. Hands typically lacked digits, or segments of them. Intact fingers were bent, twisted, bruised. Nails were smashed, blackened, or lost altogether. Faces were leathery, scarred, stoic. Teeth were missing, often rows of them. An occasional eye socket was hollow, or held an eerie glass substitute. Every face was bearded. The men lowered their heavy bulks onto the benches, snatched up knives, forks, spoons, dismantled Edith's towers, waited to be fed, whickering and pawing at the floor like horses in a stable.

Mrs. Keckonius ordered the coffee served. Edith, Perdie, and Hero carried in the steaming pitchers, poured out the dark, scalding liquid, knowing full well the loggers wouldn't drink their first cupfuls. Instead the men cradled the cups a moment, warming their hands, then, as if on cue, spilled the contents out onto the floor. Edith and her sisters scrambled to refill the cups before they cooled. The men guzzled the hot coffee as if their tongues, throats, and stomachs were made of cast iron.

Next came the food: fried meat, biscuits, flapjacks, scrambled eggs, oatmeal. The men shoveled it into their mouths, no grace, no pleases, no thank-you's, no words of any kind. They ate like dogs, heads bowed, slurping, lapping, growling. Maple syrup, melted butter, sausage grease dribbled into their beards. The flunkies hustled about, removing empty platters, replacing them, refilling cups, keeping their hands clear of the men's mouths.

When the whistle blew, indicating the speeder was ready to take the men out to the woods, forks and knives clattered deafeningly on plates. The men drained the dregs of their coffee, then a hundred-plus cups clinked in their saucers. The loggers rose in a mass, jerked a hundred-plus napkins from their collars, tossed them on their plates, retrieved their coats and hats, stuffed their cheeks with fresh plugs of snoose. The lack of compliments to the chef was a tribute: Mrs. Keckonius only heard from them when they were dissatisfied.

Sonny, another of the Smith "brothers," flashed Edith a smile as he tugged on his coat. At sixteen, he was the youngest, greenest logger, and arguably the happiest. Sonny had always hated camp work—floor scrubbing, griddle scouring, privy cleaning. He much preferred working outdoors. He told Edith that the day he was promoted to whistle punk was his release from prison.

Edith smiled back at him, not knowing whether to envy or pity his going out to the woods. Instead she prayed that he'd return that evening in one piece.

The men boarded the open boxcar behind the speeder, what they called the crummy. The whistle blew again. The speeder hissed, blew steam, chugged away.

Back in the cookhouse, the flunkies were given five minutes to swallow a plateful of leftovers before the cleanup began. The sisters' first job was to scrub the coffee off the floor. Then came the monumental task of washing the dishes. After that, the flunkies were dispatched to scrub the bunkhouses and privies, to tend to the chickens, pigs, and cows—or "slow elk," as the loggers called them. Then the supper prep began, which lasted until the men came in from the woods. Cleanup, including more backbreaking hours of dishwashing, began when the last man left the mess hall. Edith was made to stay later than the others as punishment for being late that morning. She was given the unenviable task of cleaning out the snoose pots.

When finally she was dismissed, she tramped through the mist along the plank causeways toward the flunkies' bunkhouse. The air was sodden as an old salt, as her father used to say. The bunkhouse had two doors leading to two rooms, one of them the sisters', the other, the brothers'.

"I shut it," Hero snapped when Edith stepped inside. "You mop it up."

She pointed at a puddle under the window, the window where the gull had appeared, the window Edith had left open all day. Edith fetched a towel, kneeled, sponged up the water.

"If I told, you'd get a whippin'," Hero said, standing above her.

"True," Edith said.

"Remember I didn't, then. Remember you owe me, *Dusty*."

Edith's cheeks burned. Hero settled on the nickname only days after Edith's arrival at the camp, due to Edith's having been assigned the dusty job of cleaning out the camp's woodstoves. Considering the contempt breathed into it, the nickname itself was mild, even dull-witted, yet it stung more than Edith ever let on. Hero, perhaps sensing this, persisted in its use. What she couldn't know was that Edith had been called the name as long as she could remember.

Edith had been born with a rasp to her voice, a dustiness that led to the nickname. When later she spent a great deal of her time at the stables where she and her mother kept their horses, the sobriquet stuck for good. Her mother said it fondly, in her highbred Easterner voice, the syllables swift and chipper, the *t* clicking instead of thudding, like a Westerner's, like Edith's, like Hero's. Her father said it wryly, though fondly, in his faint Irish brogue.

There was no fondness in the way Hero said it.

"I'll remember," Edith said.

"See you do," Hero said. "An' I din't tell 'bout yer sittin' on yer bunk starin' out the winda when ya shoulda been in the cookhouse, neither. So that's *two* times ya owe me."

Edith stood, walked to the basin, wrung out the towel. Hero shoved her into the basin. The water sloshed.

"Hear me, *Dusty*?" she said.

Edith spun around. "Hear you? How could I not? It's like there's a gull in here."

Perdie giggled in her bunk.

"You shut yer ugly face, Perdita Smith," Hero snapped.

Perdie's smile buckled.

"Tell you what, Hero," Edith said. "I won't tell Mother Smith that un-Christian thing you just said to your sister, and I'll just owe you one time." She tasted sourness on her tongue.

"That's tellin' her, Edith!" Perdie said, bouncing a bit on her mattress.

"You owe me *plenty*," Hero said. "An' there'll be a reck'nin', jest you wait an' see."

A bell chimed outside.

"Lights out," Perdie said, diving into her pillow.

"Sweet dreams, Hero," Edith said. She puffed out the candle on the dresser.

"You can go to hell, Edith Smith!" Hero snarled through the silver smoke.

"I'll keep that to myself as well," Edith said. "Which makes us even."

Hero fumed, said nothing, stomped away to her bunk.

Edith looked back at the window where the gull had entered. The light outside was fading, the rain falling harder. Blue light glowed on the dresser, on Edith's hairbrush. Something in the bristles, something dark and round—a burr, a seed capsule— glistened in the light. She was always brushing such things from her hair: leaves, twigs, petals, webs, dead bugs. With thumb and forefinger, she plucked out the capsule, felt its tiny spines clinging to her skin, held it up to the dusky light. It was the size of a ripe black-berry. She prized it open with her thumbnails. Out poured a quantity of seeds, dark and silky, as if covered in fine hairs, like the mink in Edith's mother's furs.

Edith knew a thing or two about seeds. Her interest in plants had been kindled when she started giving serious thought to what to feed Pippin, her horse, when it became important to her to be able to distinguish between different sorts of hays, grasses, and clovers. The interest became a hobby. She even pondered taking up horticulture as a good, solid field of study should her dream of becoming a professional equestrienne fall through.

She'd never seen any seeds like those in her palm before. They reminded her most of *corylus*, hazel.

"What in hell you doin'?" Hero hissed.

"Praying, Sister Hero," Edith replied.

Hero grumbled, rolled over, faced the wall.

Edith eased open the top right drawer—her drawer—dropped the seeds into the rusty tin can in which she saved things: old brown glass, crockery shards, shells, sawteeth, arrowheads, rusty nuts, bolts, nails, and her mother's silver-plated hoof-pick. The pick was in the shape of a horse's head, its eye, a genuine diamond. It was the only thing that remained of Edith's previous existence.

She pushed the drawer shut with her hip, crawled into her bunk beneath Perdie's. Muffled voices and the sound of roughhousing came through the wall.

"Knock it off, fellas," Sonny said. "You heard the bell. Git ta sleep."

"You ain't the bull here, jack," complained Jed, Sonny's younger, flesh-and-blood, brother.

"Oh, no?" Sonny said. "Wanna see my horns?"

There was more grunting, cursing, bumps against the wall, then Sonny spoke again.

"Good night, you shorthorns."

"Who you callin' a shorthorn?" Mickey shot back.

Edith covered her head with her pillow.

Hours later she was still awake, listening to the rain, when loggers passed by her window, yelling and laughing, stumbling over the causeways, falling into the mud. She knew beneath their slickers they wore their fine Saturday-night suits, knew they were drunk as skunks.

One of them drawled, "Brother, give me a little

canned heat and an armful of slackpullers and I'm one happy timberbeast! One happy timberbeast!"

The loggers had a language all their own. Canned heat, Edith knew, was what the men had been drinking. A slackpuller, she further knew, was a chippie, a harlot, "a woman of easy virtue," as Mother Smith put it. The voice belonged to a man called Book, who was as stout as a cedar stump and, when sober, just as talkative.

The loggers stumbled away. The stillness returned. Edith fell asleep, puzzling over the mysterious ways of men.

CHAPTER
TWO

Edith did not know if God existed somewhere above the rain, but was glad nonetheless for the Smiths' observance of His seventh day. It wasn't exactly a day of rest. Holy day or no holy day, folks and livestock had to eat. But the flunkies were relieved from breakfast duty. Not only would the loggers not need the morning meal—the crew didn't go out to the woods on Sundays—but they wouldn't be up anyway, not after spending the night drinking and carousing. Instead of showing up in the cookhouse, the flunkies were required to go to the pool hall on Sunday mornings.

The preacher, a dithered old man called Father Grimes, took the train in to deliver two sermons, one in the pool hall for the bachelors, one in the chapel for the prune pickers—the loggers with families. Then he hopped a train to camps farther up the line: Camp Ten, Eleven, Twelve . . .

Edith couldn't help believing that the sermons, which were mostly about sin and temptation, were pitched to the wrong crowd, that the men who'd benefit most from them were in bed nursing hangovers. She had trouble putting her faith in a god who saw fit to rob children of their parents and allow those heartbroken orphans to fall into the clutches of people like the Smiths. Even so, she prayed. She prayed because she had to believe there was a place people went when they died, a place reachable by those left behind, a heaven where souls reunited, where Edith could be with her mother again.

When the sermon ended that morning, the flunkies were ordered to the cookhouse to help Mrs.

Keckonius prepare the midday dinner, another event that occurred only on the sabbath. Edith passed among the men as they loitered around the camp, sipping coffee, playing poker, holding their aching heads. After dinner, the flunkies took their weekly showers, then reported to the Smiths' house.

On the Sundays Father Smith was away on business, which was most of them, the flunkies ate with Mrs. Keckonius in the mess hall, as they did every other meal during the week. But the Sundays he was home, the flunkies ate their evening dinner in the Smiths' house with their "parents." The flunkies were not allowed in the house except for these Sunday repasts. The house had a pitched cedar-shingle roof, shutters on the windows, polished maple floors, a teak secretary, a nest of tables with intricate scrollwork, a red chaise longue, imported rugs, velvet drapes, framed paintings on the walls, a piano, and a door-bell.

Orson Smith, the camp superintendent, the "push," sat at his customary spot at the head of the table. He and the preacher were the only clean-shaven men in camp. Mr. Smith wore his thinning, graying hair slicked back, parted crisply down the middle. On his nose he wore metal-framed nippers that magnified his eyes to disturbing dimensions. His lower lip was oddly full; when clasped over the upper, as it often was, it lent him a smug yet pugnacious air. He wore a tailored wool suit complete with vest, fob, and pocket watch. His pear-shaped body leaned forward as he spoke. At table, only he was permitted to speak freely. The others, including his wife, were restricted to civilities such as "Thank you," "Yes, sir," "No, sir," "Pass the potatoes, please," and "I promise it won't happen again, sir."

Mother Smith sat at the foot of the table, the three girls along one side, the three boys along the other. Jed, who despised sitting and loathed silence, was made to sit at Father Smith's left in an effort to reduce his "incessant fidgeting." Mickey, Jed's partner in mischief, sat at the opposite end, at Mother Smith's right. Mickey was small for nine, with sticks for limbs and a wide, flat, freckled face. Edith thought he looked like a leprechaun. Mickey was the architect of the pair's devilry. He once convinced Jed to shinny up to the top of a towering fir that Mickey subsequently chopped down with an ax, providing Jed with the ride of his life, as well as a broken collarbone.

Mickey adored Mother Smith to the point of coming to blows with anyone who spoke ill of her, including Jed. According to Perdie, who was Edith's chief, though dubious, source of information on the flunkies, Mickey was abandoned the day he was born, left in a tin washtub on the Smiths' doorstep. He was never told this and grew up believing he was the Smiths' only flesh-and-blood child. He saw himself as the apple of Mother Smith's eye, despite the fact that she was discernibly no kinder to him than to any of the others.

Across from Mickey, at Mother Smith's left, sat Hero. Edith assumed that Mother Smith, well aware of Hero's coquettishness, wanted her as far away from her husband as possible. This tactic did not prevent Hero from flashing Father Smith toothy grins and coy glances. Of late, however, Hero had been decidedly sulky, bordering on rude, at table. Both Father and Mother Smith appeared to be taking pains to ignore this, which Edith found quite at odds with their natures.

Edith sat at Father Smith's right elbow, with Perdie at her right. Sonny—whom the Smiths called by his given name, Amnon—was positioned between the two imps.

As second helpings were being taken, Mickey asked Hero to please pass him the gravy. Hero responded by nudging the gravy boat half an inch with her knuckle. Mother Smith looked to Father Smith, who feigned indifference.

"Your brother asked you for the gravy, Hero," Mother Smith said. "Would you kindly oblige him?"

"He c'n reach it," Hero said.

Mother Smith looked again to her husband. He stiffened in his chair under her glare.

"Hero, please hand the gravy to your brother," he said, with less authority than usual.

Hero turned gradually toward him, her eyes narrowing to slits.

Shocked at the brazenness of this defiance, Edith

looked meaningfully across the table at Sonny. He shrugged, mouthed, *"What?"*

"Gimme the gravy, Hero!" Mickey hollered.

"Mickey, I advise you to keep a civil tongue in your head," Father Smith said in a more familiarly stentorian tone.

"May I be excused?" Hero said.

"Why, Hero?" Father Smith said.

Hero stood up fast, tipping her chair over backward. It clattered onto the floor. She had everyone's attention now, even the boys'.

"I'm sick to my stomach, that's why," she sneered. *"Sir."*

Father Smith's upper lip disappeared behind his lower one. He avoided looking at his wife, who was staring right through him. "You may be excused," was all he said. He resumed his meal.

Hero marched to the front door, every step a statement.

"When you are well, however," Father Smith said to his plate, "I expect you to regain a ladylike decorum."

25

Hero went through the door, slammed it behind her.

An awkward silence came over the table. The flunkies peeked at each other, daring not to move.

"Such insolence in such a pretty girl," Father Smith said. "Must have gotten it from her mother."

According to Perdie, Hero's father had been both a logger and a family man—a prune picker—at a time when most lumbermen were bachelors. Hero was born in Camp Nine, run by the childless Orson and Idelfa Smith. A falling log crushed her father's chest when Hero was five. Her mother, a former school-marm, died soon after, the loss of her husband too much to bear, Perdie said. No other kinfolk made a claim on Hero, so the Smiths took her in. It was their first adoption.

"Mother Smith," Father Smith said to his wife, "I don't think you are doing all you can to rein that girl in."

Mother Smith rose from her chair, dropped her napkin on her seat, said, "Excuse me, but I'm all in," walked away, shut herself into the bedroom.

"Looks like a mutiny," Father Smith said, trying to act bemused. "I think dinner has come to an end, children. Clear away these things, then get back to the kitchen." He stood, wiped his mouth with his napkin, adjusted the spectacles on his nose. "I'll be leaving tonight and will be gone for some time. Obey Mother Smith."

"Yes, sir," they all said.

Father Smith walked away to his library, shut himself in.

Jed cheered soundlessly, shook his fists over his head, whispered, "Last one out's a dirty hoosier!"

If the flunkies cleaned up quickly after Sunday dinner, they were given an hour furlough before beginning the supper prep, an hour to do what they liked, an hour they dreamed of all week long.

"Go on, you kids," Mrs. Keckonius said when they'd finished that night. "Clear out. Be back in an hour."

Mickey and Jed whooped, yanked off their aprons, burst out the door. Sonny fetched his fiddle, joined in with a band playing reels outside one of the bunkhouses. Hero danced to the music, twirled her tattered Mother Hubbard for them, peered at the men teasingly out of the corners of her eyes. Edith ran to the sisters' room, pulled open her drawer, plucked out the furry seeds from her can.

"Whatcha got?" Perdie asked, coming up behind her, startling her.

"Seeds," she said. "Some funny seeds." She closed her fingers over them. "Come on."

Perdie trailed Edith across the wobbly planks to the railroad spur that led out of camp. The sun was out, but wasn't hot. Raindrops streaked the sky, sparkling like tinsel, tickling the girls' faces. The rain paid no mind to the sun in that part of the world, fell from gray skies or blue. Edith and Perdie followed the tracks until the woodsmoke of the camp no longer clung to them, the stench of sewage pits, slop holes, livestock, the rendering shed, and the refuse burner no longer assaulted their nostrils.

Edith peered back over her shoulder at the green mountains rising high above the camp, many of them partially shorn of trees, some shaved bald, others with peaks encrusted with glaciers. She surveyed the shoddy, battleship-gray bunkhouses, the crooked privies, the clotheslines with flapping long johns, the piles of junk, all arranged without rhyme or reason. The camp, like the hobo jungles back home, had been built to be abandoned and forgotten. It was nobody's home. Even the cluster of family houses at the edge of camp, with its community meeting hall and one-room schoolhouse (which the flunkies had neither the time nor invitation to attend) were ramshackle, temporary, rootless. The vegetable gardens were sparse and nubby, the covered porches slapped on like afterthoughts. The little stand of trees spared by the company for shade looked less like a grove, more like an oversight. Like the wasteland around it, the camp would be struck when no longer lucrative and stripped of anything of value—including the shade trees.

"What ya stoppin' fer?" Perdie said, tugging at Edith's elbow.

They continued on, past the drab fields of kindling that had not long before been a dense forest, past spindly snags poking up like the bones of dead birds, sawed-off stumps broad enough for a grown man to make a bed of, others big enough for the man to invite his wife and children in with him and have room for his dog at his feet. Edith recalled black-and-white pictures in *Life* magazine of soldiers in the Great War lying amid similar scenes of destruction, their limbs blown off, their bodies broken and charred, their faces smeared with black blood.

"Shame what they've done here," she said aloud.

"What'd they do?" Perdie asked, looking around.

"They chopped down the trees. Chopped down the forest."

"They can chop it all down s'far as I'm concerned," Perdie said. "I don't like the woods. They're spooky."

They walked on till they came to the pitchfork-shaped hemlock snag, where they always turned left. Moisture seeped through the cracks in Edith's galoshes, through the holes in her shoes, and soaked her socks.

"My feet are wet," Perdie said.

Edith smiled with compassion. "Almost there."

"We're goin' to your ma's tree, huh?"

Edith nodded.

She had replanted the hazel branch from her backyard in a large, hollow cedar stump, choosing that spot because the soil was darker, richer, less desiccated than that around it. Edith put this down to the decaying of the stump itself: It enriched the soil as it decomposed. Edith chose to believe the tree had fallen before the loggers had gotten to it, that it had collapsed of its own accord, lived out its life, and that it was now giving new life to the hazel branch. The branch looked feeble amid such desolation, yet it thrived. It had pluck—a word Cathleen, Edith's mother, often winkingly used in describing herself.

"Your ma drown'ded, didn't she?" Perdie asked, sitting on the edge of the stump.

Edith nodded, knowing that Perdie wasn't really asking, that she knew the answer, that she was only making sure she was thinking the right thoughts. Perdie often belittled herself for thinking the wrong thoughts and doing the wrong things, often told herself "I'm so stupid" or "I'm such a moron." Edith believed this was due to Mother Smith, the way the woman always picked at Perdie despite knowing how hard Perdie took such things, how hard Perdie was on herself. Mother Smith surely knew Perdie's history, knew why Perdie would likely blame herself for things.

As with the others, all Edith knew of Perdie's story she'd learned from Perdie. When she was six, her father, a banker in the same seaport city where Edith was born and raised, one day stepped in front of a train on the way home from work, leaving Perdie alone with her grief-stricken mother, who blamed herself for the tragedy. This, Perdie asserted, was a mistake. Her father was driven to end his life, she said, not by his perfect and beautiful wife, but by his ugly and worthless daughter.

After her husband's death, Perdie's mother began to act strangely, flapping her arms like some great bird, spinning like a top, lolling her head as if she'd lost control of it, cussing, raging, arguing with herself. Later she was committed to a mental hospital. For this Perdie also blamed herself. With her mother in the hospital, Perdie was then handed over to the Smiths.

Edith sometimes imagined the Smiths sitting at their breakfast table, scouring the day's obituaries for surviving children, for free labor.

"An' yer pa left," Perdie said, her eyes on the branch.

"Yeah," Edith said.

"An' you was all alone?"

"Except for the horses," Edith said.

"Pippin."

"Right."

"An' yer ma's."

"Emma."

"An' they made ya sell 'em when they found ya, din't they?"

"They sold everything."

"What'd they do with the money?"

Edith looked at her, waited.

"I know," Perdie said. "They paid off yer pa's debts cuz he jes' sailed away on his boat."

"And I was sent here," Edith said.

"How long was you alone after yer pa left?"

Edith smiled.

"A month, right?" Perdie said.

Edith nodded.

"Whadya eat?"

"The little food we had around."

"What about Pippin an' Emma?"

"I fed them vegetables from the garden."

"Horses like carrots, huh?"

"Mm-hm."

"Was you scairt bein' by yerself?"

"Sad, mostly," Edith said. "And lonesome."

"But you had the horses fer comp'ny."

"Yeah."

"Wish I had me a horse."

Edith slid her arm around Perdie's waist, leaned against her shoulder.

"When Ma's better she'll come an' get me," Perdie said. "I'll make her take ya with us."

"Thanks," Edith said. She scooped the seeds from her pocket, looked them over in her palm.

"What sort are they?" Perdie asked.

"I don't know," Edith said.

She dug a shallow trench around the hazel branch, dropped in the seeds, spaced them evenly, covered them over, tamped down the dirt, let the soft rain slowly rinse the dirt from her fingers.

"Can ya tell me the story again?" Perdie asked shyly.

"Sure," Edith said.

They sat down together on one of the stump's knobby roots and Edith once more unfolded the tragic tale of her mother, Cathleen Cade Kelly, self-proclaimed pampered pig-iron princess, heiress to a fortune in steel, musical prodigy, accomplished equestrienne. Cathleen was witty, urbane, ebullient, polyglot, beautiful (flaxen hair, alabaster complexion, eyes like sapphires). She was raised in the lap of luxury, fed from a silver spoon, loved by all, courted by many, destined for a brilliant future. Over the many retellings, Edith had carefully refined this description, mixing in her mother's own heavily embellished autobiography with elements from the novels Cathleen read and reread, and read aloud to Edith, the novels of Balzac, the Brontës, Jane Austen, and Edith Wharton, Edith's namesake. What was true in Cathleen's story and what was made up had become harder and harder to discern. Nevertheless it had evolved into a tale worthy of retelling, a tale straight out of one of Cathleen's tragic romances. Edith preferred it this way: The more it resembled fiction, the less real it seemed.

Princess Cathleen met a sailor with fiery eyes, fiery hair, and a fiery disposition. Billy Kelly by name, he was the sole survivor of a family felled by the influenza and had been sent to live with a cold-hearted widow aunt, who resented the imposition. At eighteen, Billy came into a surprise inheritance (his parents had fortuitously taken out life insurance policies on themselves), most of which he promptly squandered on a creaky old ketch, the *Stormy Petrel*, though he'd been to sea but once, back when he sailed over the ocean from Dublin tucked snugly inside the womb of his dear mother. He blew the rest of his inheritance sailing around the world.

"He had fiery eyes?" Perdie asked, on cue.

"*Once*," Edith answered, cryptically as ever.

The princess and the sailor met on the streets of New York City, bumping into each other as she stepped out of a boutique. He was literally knocked off his feet, laid flat by shopping bags "mighty as the north wind," as he would come to repeat. Sincerest apologies were exchanged, followed by cups of coffee obliviously sipped in a handy coffee shop. Eyelashes were fluttered, tattoos flashed, fingers brushed, a walk along the waterfront suggested, an armful of flowers from a peddler spontaneously purchased, an invitation to board the ketch offered, the lateness of the hour realized, a first kiss fumbled through, then, two days later, a proposal of marriage accepted.

Perdie gasped here, breathed her line: "A whirlwind romance!"

Edith nodded with requisite dreaminess, continued:

Cathleen's mother wept copiously when the besotted lovebirds delivered the news. Her father exploded. He threatened to disown Cathleen if she didn't immediately break off the engagement. Billy flew into a rage, roaring that he would not be looked down upon, then stormed out. Cathy—as only Billy

37

ever called her—chased after him amid a chorus of protest. They were wed the next morning at City Hall, with Billy's first mate, a man of shadowy background known only as Skinty, bearing witness. They then set sail for a tropical honeymoon.

Cathy learned to sail along the way, learned to love it, added it to the long list of things that came easily to her. Skinty, witnessing the blossoming of an able seawoman, read the writing on the wall, abandoned ship in the Virgin Islands, saying "Two's company, three's a crowd." Besides, he had found his earthly paradise.

The bride and bridegroom sailed on without him, Cathy rising in rank to first mate. Billy told her his dream of a life at sea, the wayfaring life, each day a new port, a new land, a new horizon. Cathy liked the lilt of it.

"You sailed with your pa, too, din't ya?" Perdie asked.

"Many times," Edith replied, playing up her wistfulness.

"My pa was 'fraida the water," Perdie said. "Never set foot in a boat in his life. Neither have I."

"It's not for everybody," Edith said.

Perdie nodded.

The newlyweds had no money, but got by on what Billy could scrape together doing odd jobs during the *Petrel*'s periodic dry-dock refurbishments. Sometimes they took rich tourists on cruises, where Cathleen's grace and erudition, not to mention her facility with languages, proved to be assets. They ate so much fish that Cathleen joked gills were forming behind her ears.

A month before their first anniversary, Cathleen, her belly ballooning, set down her tattered copy of *Ethan Frome* and said, "It's time, Billy." He steered the ketch at full sail to the nearest port. Edith was delivered belowdecks a few minutes shy of midnight on the last day of September, with a seasick midwife attending. The next morning, Cathleen announced that her seafaring days were over, that she needed solid ground beneath her feet and the baby's cradle.

"She can't learn to crawl on the deck of a ship, husband," she told Billy.

"I'm the one learnt ta crawl," Billy would later quip.

He took a job, the first of his life, on a fishing boat. This was akin to dressing a logger in overalls, to corralling a mustang. The family rented a small place, fixed up the rundown carriage house out back so Cathleen could give music and French lessons. She had no takers for Latin. In time, as their fortunes grew, they bought the rental house, then a horse for Cathleen, then one for ten-year-old Edith. They stabled them out of town.

Edith learned to ride Eastern, though she later switched to Western, feeling it suited her better. Cathleen said she had good hands, which thrilled Edith. She'd always hidden from view what she considered to be ridiculously large mitts. The family carved out a happy little place for themselves in their adoptive seaport city, despite the palpable dimming of Billy's fire.

Then came the crash. Cathleen's father, ruined, let himself into his building one Saturday, rode the elevator to his quiet office, mounted his oaken desk, and hung himself with an electrical cord. Cathleen, having been disowned and disinherited, learned of it in the morning paper. She telegraphed her mother, but never received a response. A week later, her mother swallowed a fistful of sleeping pills and never woke.

Here Edith paused, for here the story drew perilously close to Perdie's own.

"My pa killed hisself," Perdie said. "It was cuzza the crash, too, Ma says."

"I know," Edith said.

"But it wudn't the crash. It was me."

"No. It was the crash. Now quiet and let me finish."

Cathleen sank into dark moods: Didn't read, didn't ride, wouldn't teach. No one could afford lessons anymore, anyway. Billy was forced to take a cut in pay, then another, then was let go. Bill collectors crawled out of the woodwork. Cathleen refused to sell the horses, took a job slinging hash at a diner to pay the stable fees. Billy wouldn't sell the ketch, took to drinking nights at the pub with his mates, then took to drinking afternoons as well. Later Edith and her mother converted Cathleen's studio into a small stable, brought the horses home.

Shantytowns had sprung up at the edges of the city.

The streets teemed with the down-and-out, the hungry, the desperate.

"These hard times can't last," Cathleen reassured Edith.

But they did. They went on for years. It was the saddest period of Edith's life . . . up till then.

Then one day Cathleen developed a pain in her shoulder, the cause of which no doctor could fathom.

"From carrying blue-plate specials," she joked.

Another waitress at the diner told her of a man on a nearby island, an herbalist, a "genius," who'd done wonders for the waitress's sciatica. Cathleen started seeing him once a week. Several months into her treatment, on a cold, rainy tenth of January, a ferry returning from the island was swallowed by a dense fog and collided with a tug pulling a barge. While the passengers were being escorted onto lifeboats, the ferry lurched, listed, capsized, then sank into the frigid water. Several passengers did not make it to shore, Cathleen among them.

"She drown'ded," Perdie said.

"That's what they told us," Edith said.

"An' yer pa left."

Edith nodded.

"How old was ya?"

"Fifteen, same as now."

"An' ya lived alone with Pippin an' Emma."

"That's right."

"Ya even slept with 'em, din't ya?"

"Uh-huh."

"Wish I had me a horse," Perdie sighed. "If'n I did, I'd ride off an' find Ma. You could come with."

"If wishes were horses . . ." Edith began.

"Beggars'd ride," Perdie finished.

Edith stood up. "We better get back."

"Thanks fer the story," Perdie said.

"Anytime," said Edith.

CHAPTER
Three

In the middle of setting the tables for supper, Edith gave in to the urge that had nagged her all week: She slipped away from camp and ran along the tracks to her hollow cedar stump. The seeds hadn't sprouted. Edith sighed her disappointment, then chastened herself for her childish dreams, for believing the gull was a heavenly emissary bearing magical, beanstalk-like seeds, instead of accepting that she had merely brushed them out of her ratty hair. The sound of the speeder steaming by reminded her she was truant.

When Edith arrived, a crowd was mobbing the crummy, which had been disconnected from the speeder and hooked up to the lokie. Everyone was there: Mother Smith, Mrs. Keckonius, the loggers, the flunkies, the prune pickers' wives and children, the timekeeper, the bathhouse attendants. Most surprising were the loggers. Why hadn't they rushed to the showers, to the bunkhouses, to supper? Instead they stood like statues, their jaws slack, shoulders slumped, eyes haunted. Had a logger been badly hurt? Killed? What else could cause such hubbub? A wave of panic shook Edith: Was it *Sonny*? She scanned the crowd, didn't see him, spied Jed and Mickey, hustled up behind them, jerked at Jed's elbow.

"Watch it!" he said, spinning around.

"Is it Sonny?" she demanded.

"Sonny?" Mickey said. "Nah, some squirrel name a' Fitz. Darn fool cut through his own safety rope. Fell a hunnert feet. Smashed his bones to powder." A smile flirted at his lips. "S'pose he's Flat Fitz now."

Jed snorted.

Edith swallowed hard, tried to mask her relief. She

shouldn't feel relieved, she knew, not with a man lying in there cold and broken. She ached at not being able to put a face to his name.

She felt a tap on her shoulder, turned. It was Sonny. She blinked, wiped her tears on her sleeve.

"Was Fitz married?" she asked him.

Sonny shook his head. "He slep' in the same bunkhouse as me. Nice fella. Kinda quiet. Quieter now, I guess."

"You had to ride in with him?"

"Not jes' that. He fell early this mornin'. Been lyin' out there dead the whole day."

That explains the men's stricken expressions, Edith thought.

"Did you see it happen?" she asked.

"Heard it. He cussed all the way down. Wasn't as loud as I'd a' guessed when he hit. Nowhere near as loud as a tree, 'course."

Edith watched him as he spoke, scrutinized his long nose, short chin, the mass of freckles, the rusty hair, those ridiculous ears, too small at twice their size, his emerald eyes—like her father's—that perpetually blinked, as if there were perpetually some foreign object in them. Handsome was not the word that came to Edith's mind while looking at Sonny, though neither was homely.

"I'm glad you're a whistle punk," she said.

"Yeah. Won't be fallin' out of no tree, leastways."

"They just let him lie out there all day? Didn't they try to help him?"

Sonny shrugged. "He was past helpin', an' the bull, he's got logs t' yard. Sure was queer out there, though. The men were actin' funny. Lookin' in. Made you worry. A fella can't let his mind go wanderin' off on a show. A hunnert ways to get it out there when you're payin' *close* attention."

Accidents in the woods were far from uncommon. A man called Eyedog had lost an arm—and consequently his job—under a rolling log just the week before. But Fitz was the first man killed since Edith's arrival at the camp.

She felt an impulse, like everyone else, to peek into the crummy, to look upon the man whose life had left him, but it passed. She had seen corpses before, had gone to the morgue with her father, had been made to look at unidentified bodies fished out of the harbor, had been asked if any of them were her mother. She'd resented having to do this, especially after gazing upon the parade of hideous, swollen bodies.

What's more, she had not believed the police when they told her that Cathleen had drowned, that she was dead. There was no evidence that she had been on the ferry, despite several survivors' vague memories of seeing her on board. Cathleen was striking. You either saw her or you didn't. Though it was true she had disappeared, Edith never doubted that her brave, resourceful mother had survived, that she'd reappear when least expected, gaily waving, then wildly embellishing the account of her survival.

When that failed to occur, Edith fell back on other, Cathleenesque narratives: Like Jonah, she was swallowed by a whale, surviving on the whale's catch while devising her escape; she was stranded on a desert island, like Crusoe, concocting ways to attract the attention of passing ships; she was adrift upon flotsam, spearing her meals with a jerry-built harpoon.

What was impossible was the prospect of Cathleen being found bloated and blue like those specimens—not people, not any longer—in the morgue. If indeed she'd drowned, she surely had been taken far out to sea, where her body had provided nourishment for marine life of all kinds; she had become part of the sea.

If she'd drowned . . . *if, if, if* . . . she would not have been afraid but elated, for at the end she would have been visited by a multitude of gulls. Gulls always flocked to such scenes. Billy detested gulls, found them greedy and obnoxious scavengers, but Cathleen loved them. She called them angels of the sea. She would have loved to depart among them, Edith thought.

The lokie roared to life, blew her whistle. The crowd stepped back. The train pulled out.

"All right, you flunkies!" Mrs. Keckonius yelled. "Git back t' the kitchen! We got supper t' git on the table!"

Sonny smiled a good-bye to Edith, headed off toward the bunkhouse. The flunkies fell in behind

Mrs. Keckonius. Mother Smith brought up the rear.

"D'ya see 'im?" Mickey said to Jed. "Beard all full a' dried blood!"

"Have some respect for the dead, boy," Mrs. Keckonius snapped. "It'll be you one day."

"Yes, ma'am," Mickey said, then he and Jed snickered behind her back.

In the kitchen Hero said in a voice loud enough for Mother Smith to hear, "So where'd *you* run off to, Edith?"

"Yes, Edith," Mother Smith said, scowling. "We all looked for you."

Edith stared at her adoptive mother, stunned at how lightly she brushed aside the death of a fellow human being, as if a life lost were nothing more than a momentary imposition, like a cow on the tracks. Idelfa Smith was a woman of fewer years than her appearance suggested, a woman whose every worry was etched into her face. Creases fanned out from the corners of her mouth, from the corners of her eyes, guttered her brow. Her mouth was an unlucky horseshoe: open end down. Her eyes were so pale it was hard to tell what color they were. None of the ways the flunkies described her—mean, cruel, wicked—captured the woman's essence the way the word weary did. Mother Smith was worn to a frazzle. Hero swore she was frigid, giving that as the reason the Smiths adopted children, as well as why Father Smith was so rarely around. Edith could not know if any of this were true, but it did seem true that at least part of Mother Smith was very cold indeed.

The woman set her hands on her hips. "Well, Edith?" she said.

"A man's dead," Edith said, stiffening her spine, taking advantage of the extra couple of inches in height she had. "What does it matter where I was?"

"We haven't time for this, Mrs. Smith," Mrs. Keckonius said. "We got hungry men comin'."

Mother Smith bristled, stomped off.

"She's been awful tetchy these days," Mrs. Keckonius said. "If I didn't know better, I'd say she was in a fam'ly way."

"Can't be in a fam'ly way when yer husband don't come near ya," Hero said, surprising both Edith and

Mrs. Keckonius with her ardor. "If she's got a bun in the oven, someone *else* put it there."

Mrs. Keckonius did not dignify this remark with a reply. She turned to Edith. "Set the tables," she said. "A hunnert an' three."

"But what about—" Edith began to say.

"Give him his setting. It'll be the only testament the man ever gets."

Usually the evening meal was livelier than breakfast, the men talking boisterously, laughing, arguing, sometimes breaking into song, though mostly they relived tales of the woods, many of them tall as redwoods. That night, though, the men not only didn't talk, they barely ate. They poked at their food, moved it around their plates, stared at it, or off into space, or down into their laps, or at the untouched tower of dishes at place setting number fifty-four.

They did drink coffee, however. Edith, Perdie, and Hero bustled about the tables, refilling their cups. In some of them Edith detected the scent of spirits.

Some of the men had brought their flasks to the table. Liquor was legal again, but it was strictly forbidden in camp. According to Father Smith, drinking and logging didn't mix.

As usual Hero lingered nearest the younger, handsomer loggers, casting glances their way, batting her long lashes, thrusting out her young bosom, slinking her hips. It galled her that the men, lost inside their heads, failed to notice.

She did impress one man, Mr. Prescod, the foreman, who was neither young nor handsome. Once, as Hero passed behind him, he reached back and untied her apron strings. At first she affected pique, then, seeing who it was, dealt him the real thing.

"Mitts off, chum!" she said.

The men looked up. Prescod's face reddened.

"Yer even purdier when yer angry," he said.

"An' yer even uglier when yer disgustin'!"

To Hero's delight, a rumble of laughter arose from the men. Prescod was not amused. "Clam up, you stiffs!" he barked, standing up.

They did. The men were real Paul Bunyans, but

the bull of the woods could snap off their livelihoods with the stroke of a pen. With loggers losing their jobs every day, laughing at the boss could land a man in a breadline.

Mrs. Keckonius came into the mess hall later, wagged her finger, hollered, "You fellas got some complaint to make, cuz I got grub in there goin' to waste!"

The men shook their heads, mumbled negatives.

"It's Fitz, then," the cook said.

The hulks shrugged their huge shoulders, hung their heads.

"Hell, he was a logger. He knew the risks. Now he's dead, God bless 'im, but you ain't. You all got to go back out there in the mornin', so you better eat, less'n you'd like to join ol' Fitz in the cold, cold ground. Do as I say, now. Don't no one leaves Maggie Keckonius's food on the table." She walked back to the kitchen.

The men grudgingly lifted their forks, filled their mouths, worked their jaws, struggled to swallow.

The cook returned later.

"All right, you cows! Enough grazin'! Git out of my cookhouse! Go on! Scat!"

The floorboards creaked as the men rose, trudged toward the door.

The sun rose earlier as April yielded to May, and the loggers stayed up well past lights out. It still rained almost constantly, but the dampness didn't bring with it the same chill. Wildflowers bloomed in the gray stump gardens. Twenty new loggers squeezed into the bunkhouses, onto the benches in the mess hall. The work for everyone doubled with the extra daylight. Edith's droppage increased. Timber season was in full swing.

This was precisely the time—with more men, longer days, and acres of trees ripe for the ax—that the company cut the loggers' pay. Father Smith delivered the news on a Sunday, after services in the pool room. It had to be done, he assured them, it being the only way the company could afford the extra men. If they could tighten their belts now, though, he said, they'd be cut in to the windfall later. Of course, they were free to look elsewhere for a better wage; but, he reminded them, as if they needed reminding, that times were tough all over.

Not a single logger walked off the job. There was no place to go; Jacobs & Williams owned every stick for miles in any direction. There were plenty of men around who would gladly fill the boots of anyone who quit, and for less pay.

"The company's got all the aces, a fifth up its sleeve, an' a sixth in its boot," Book said.

The men worked the long stretch between sunup and sundown, did little else but sleep. An avalanche of logs rolled down the skid roads to the cold deck, got stacked into pyramids on flatcars, then hauled away. Saturday night in town even lost its luster as the long days took their toll. More men began showing up for services on Sundays in their Saturday suits, hats in their laps, hair slicked down, palms pressed together.

"Desperate times called for desperate measures," Edith overheard Mrs. Keckonius say.

When the flunkies were given their leave after cleanup one Sunday night, Edith ran from camp along the tracks. The stump gardens were expanding, the forests in the distance receding. Edith's seeds had sprouted a couple of weeks before, but had rapidly grown into an unspectacular shrub of tangled, woody, hazel-like stems, whiskered with fine black hairs. So much for magic. The little hazel branch, however, had firmly taken root. Buds on its spindly arms were primed to open. Catkins had formed: small, pendulous male ones, and smaller, acorn-shaped female ones with brilliant red stigmas. Edith sat down on the cedar stump, consoled at least by the hazel branch's success.

Edith's thoughts drifted from the stump to the stump gardens to Eyedog, the logger who had lost his arm. Before he boarded his train out of the woods, she'd overheard him tell another man that he could sometimes feel his lost hand straining to, say, turn a doorknob, or scratch an itch. Edith, too, sometimes caught herself thinking of things to tell her mother, questions to ask her, though Cathy was no longer there. But Edith had not lost a limb as Eyedog had; she had lost her mother, her source, her roots. Edith was not the stump; she was the severed limb. Like the hazel branch, like the other flunkies, she had been snapped off her family tree, taken from her home, forced to struggle for survival, a transplant in a garden of stumps. If a branch could become a tree again, she wondered, could an orphan become a person?

On the way back to camp, Sonny jumped out from behind a rotting log, startling her half to death.

"Sorry," he said, grinning, blinking. "I couldn't resist." When he saw that she had been crying, his grin faded.

"Were you following me?" Edith asked.

"No, a cougar."

"There's a cougar out here?" Edith said, alarmed.

Sonny shrugged. "Tracks, anyway. What're you doin' out here?"

"That's my business."

"Oh," Sonny said, looking at his feet. "Sorry again."

"I have to get back to the kitchen."

"I'll walk ya, if it's all right."

Edith nodded. She wanted him to.

"Are the men very angry?" she asked as they walked.

"Sure, but there ain't nuthin' they can do 'bout nuthin'." He paused, snapped a dead twig off a snag. "They sure don't like me much."

"They don't?"

"Naw. I'm takin' a man's job, an' I'm green, an' I don't draw no pay."

Edith hadn't considered any of this.

"It's still better'n bein' in camp, though," he went on. "Better'n bein' under Mother Smith's thumb. But it's funny, me achin' so bad fer so long t' get out to the woods an' now all I do all day is watch it gettin' chopped down." He looked at Edith. "You ever been in the forest?"

There were many times when Sonny reminded Edith of her father, the sailor with the fiery hair and eyes. It wasn't mere physical resemblance. Both Sonny and Billy pined desperately for things out of their grasp; both resented the constraints put on them, hid the fires in their bellies, were betrayed by the light in their eyes, the gradually dimming light.

"Deep in the forest?" he asked.

"No," she said.

"Well then, ya better hurry up, cuz it ain't gonna be aroun' much longer."

"I wonder if that's what makes the men so hard," Edith said.

"How d'ya mean?"

"Y'know, having to kill things all day."

"They're not so hard. They just put that on. Inside they're scairt. I don't think they think too much 'bout the trees bein' alive. They're too busy thinkin' 'bout keepin' their own selves alive."

They walked the rest of the way without talking, then went their separate ways in camp, both looking at each other differently than before.

Mother Smith pounced on Edith the second she stepped through the cookhouse door. She had a switch in her hand.

"You're no better than anyone else here, y'know!"

she said, her face red. Hero stood behind her, delighted, triumphant.

"I don't think that I am," Edith answered as evenly as she could.

"Mrs. Keckonius said an hour. You been gone close to two. Lean over that table."

Edith didn't move.

"Then you'll get it right here," Mother Smith yelled, bringing the switch down on the back of Edith's legs. Edith stifled a scream, attempted to shield herself from the next blow, got whipped across the forearms for her trouble. She twisted to avoid the next one, took it on the hip; it cut a slit in her dress. Mother Smith dealt her three more licks, then straightened up, set her hand on her chest as if to still her heart. Edith spat on the floor. Her saliva tasted like blood.

"Stop that spittin' in my kitchen," Mrs. Keckonius said, "an' git in here an' gut these chickens."

CHAPTER
Four

The days grew longer still, the sun resting barely six hours a night, the loggers and flunkies less than that. The speeder ride to the woods doubled as the crews chopped deeper and deeper. Then in August, during supper in the mess hall and without his customary smugness, Father Smith informed the men that, due to plummeting lumber prices, resources had to be pooled. Camp Nine would be merging with Camp Eleven up the line.

"After more than twelve years of dedicated service

to the company, I am being asked to share administrative duties with the push of Camp Eleven."

His resentment was palpable, so much so that a few of the men sniggered.

"Regardless of my feelings about it, the move is set to take place in two weeks' time."

The men by then had absorbed so much bad news, had taken so many cuts in pay, and increases in hours, witnessed so many recruits injured, even killed, that they couldn't muster any protest, or even much interest. They kept their heads bowed, silently eating Mrs. Keckonius's food, their one consolation.

After supper, Sonny led Edith outside, told her that he and Jed wouldn't be going along to the new camp.

"I got word from my pa," he said. "He wants Jed an' me to join 'im at his new farm. Yep, my pa's a hoosier."

"Your *father*?" Edith said, struggling to keep shrillness out of her voice. "When did he write? Why didn't you tell me?"

She and Sonny had been stealing away together all

summer, sneaking off on long rambles, having long talks. He told her the loggers' Bunyan stories, leaving out the racier ones. He told her about his mother, who died bringing Jed into the world. Edith identified wildflowers—tiger lilies, cat's-ears, Johnny-jump-ups—and even took him out to the cedar stump. She told him about the gull, the seeds, showed him the shrub (which had outgrown the stump, rerooted itself over and over, spread into a sprawling thicket of whiskery stems and finely bristled leaves), told him how she had childishly wished for a beanstalk. She showed him the hazel branch, told him where it had come from.

After all they had shared, his keeping a secret of such consequence from her stung.

"I only jes' got the letter," Sonny said, looking away. "Hero gave it to me when I got off the crummy yesterday."

"*Hero!*" Edith shrieked so loudly she had to cover her own mouth.

Edith had been convinced all summer that Hero was trying to sabotage things between her and Sonny:

64

Letting Mother Smith know whenever either of them slipped off; stumbling or bursting in on them "accidentally"; insulting Edith in front of him; flirting with him shamelessly. Edith took reluctant pride that, despite Hero's curls and charms, Sonny preferred plain ol', ratty-haired, flat-as-a-board Dusty Kelly. She was even beginning to believe the corny old saw about beauty being only skin deep. The problem was, Hero and her skin-deep beauty wouldn't let up.

"She saw Mother Smith goin' through her mail in the mess hall yesterday mornin'," Sonny said, "an' saw her throw a letter on the fire. After she left, Hero fished it out. The envelope was burnt, but the letter inside wudn't. It was from my pa. Hero an' me don' read so good, but 'tween us we figured out what it said."

"Why didn't you come to me for help?" Edith said, not a little hurt. "I read fine."

"I mentioned that to Hero, but she said she din't want you knowin', said you had sump'm against her an' would squeal to Mother Smith 'bout her gettin' into her mail."

"Something against *her*?" Edith said.

Sonny, clearly wanting to skip over this contentious detail, went on.

"My pa said in the letter he'd married a widow who had a farm an' he wants me an' Jed to get down there an' help him with it."

"Probably can't afford hands," Edith said, surprised at her cynicism.

"Maybe," Sonny said, surprised as well. "But I'm still thinkin' maybe me an' Jed ought to go."

The weight of it hit Edith: Sonny was leaving, for good. She didn't want him to, but she couldn't ask him to stay. She'd never ask that of anyone, even Hero. She wished they could all go.

"How will you get there?" she asked.

"We got no money, so we'll hafta hop a freight. Hobo it."

Edith pictured him and clumsy Jed running wildly along the tracks, tossing their bindles through an open boxcar door, trying to jump aboard as the train picked up speed. She shuddered, imagining their not making it, falling beneath the train.

"Sounds dangerous," she said.

"Nah. Ever'body does it these days. Kids younger'n us. That's what they say in the bunkhouses."

Edith had seen plenty of young boys, too, in the shantytowns back home. Hobo boys.

"When will you go?"

"Don't know. Soon, I guess." He looked into her eyes. His blinked like mad.

"Why do you blink so much?" she said, wanting to keep this from becoming one of her mother's tragic romances. She had never once mentioned his blinking to him.

"Blink?" he answered.

And she kissed him. It was the first time she had, and the first time she'd kissed a boy, ever. She got mostly teeth. Sonny hadn't expected it, looked flabbergasted.

Then Edith pulled back, said, "I better get back."

"You could go with us," Sonny blurted out.

Edith, thinking it was the kiss talking, shrugged, turned, ducked back inside, strode swiftly through the long mess hall, frantic thoughts racing through her head, tears pooling in her eyes, leaking onto her cheeks. She didn't notice the loggers watching her, didn't hear the bull, Prescod, scoffing, didn't see his foot edge out into her path. She hit the floor hard.

"Y'oughta be more careful, miss," Prescod said, reaching out his hand. "Here, lemme help ya up."

Edith sprang to her feet, dabbed her eyes with her apron, glared at the man. "You trip me, mister?"

"Me?" Prescod said with a laugh. A few others laughed behind him. "Why, I'd never trip a lady. Here, you lost this." He held out her boot, which had come off. Its threadbare lace was broken. "I'm your Prince Charming." Another smattering of laughter.

Edith snatched the boot. "You're a *frog*," she said.

The room erupted in laughter. Prescod's face reddened.

Hero stood at the door to the kitchen, arms akimbo, saturnine grin on her face.

"Wonder where *you* been," she said.

Edith elbowed her aside and went past.

Sunlight still glowed through the bunkhouse window at nine o'clock that night, fell on Edith lying awake on her bunk. At ten she gave up on sleep, pulled on a dress, tiptoed out. She hesitated outside the boys' room, wondering whether to give Sonny their signature rap on the wall. They often slipped out together after everyone was asleep. She usually looked forward to these late-night walks all day long, but the memory of their bumbling kiss caused her to wince. She hastened away alone.

A fog had settled on the ground, making navigating the camp tricky, but providing good cover. Edith stepped cautiously along the slick, mossy causeways, out of camp along the railroad ties, turned left at the pitchfork hemlock. The white gull, the one from before, in her room, was perched on the little hazel tree. It swiveled its head toward her, clicked its beak, screamed, opened its wings on their hinges.

"Don't go," Edith said. *"Please."*

The bird lifted off into the mist, again leaving behind a chill in Edith's bones.

Nothing stays, Edith thought. Not the gull, not

her mother, not her father, not Sonny, not even Camp Nine. Could the hazel branch survive another transplanting? Could she bear to leave it behind? She kneeled beside it, touched the place where the gull had lit, remembered the first time it had perched there: the day Edith had planted the branch in her backyard at home, after it had knocked off her father's hat. She recalled his bending down to retrieve it, his placing it back on his head, adjusting the angle, peering back over his shoulder at her, furtively, his face red. From embarrassment? From shame? It never took much to bring a blush to Billy Kelly's freckled face. He then walked away down the sidewalk. It was less than two months after the ferry accident. He did not return.

Before that day, he and Edith had been moving wordlessly about the house, making lackluster meals, barely touching them, paging through books, old newspapers, old magazines, staring out windows, at walls, into the middle distance, sleeping late, retiring early, napping all day like cats. In the beginning, friends of Cathleen's dropped by with casseroles, baked goods, and sympathy; but Billy always chased them away. He detested charity and pity. Sometimes he flew into fits of rage over the smallest of things. Other times he collapsed into weeping with something of Cathy's in his hand: A lipstick, a hat pin, her toothbrush. Perhaps because of these displays, Edith kept her grief to herself. Someone, she believed, ought to try to be strong.

The horses were her only solace in those days. She did not ride them. Their saddles, along with everything else deemed nonessential but valuable, had been sold long before the accident. She spent long hours brushing their coats, manes, and tails, cleaning their hooves with her mother's silver, diamond-studded hoof-pick in the shape of a horse's head. The studio-turned-stable out back was tiny, barely big enough for two horses side by side. When it didn't rain, Edith groomed them in the yard; when it did, she squeezed in between them in the stable, listened to their deep, nostrilly breaths, pressed her ear to their enormous rib cages, listened to their giant hearts beat. She fed them vegetables from her garden, let them graze on the lawn, commiserated with Emma, mourned with her.

Then one night at the table, with an untouched supper of chipped beef on toast and boiled potatoes before them, Billy spoke to her. Edith would not have been more surprised if Pippin had.

"I miss 'er," her father said in a meek voice. "I keep hopin' she'll come back. I keep waitin'.".

Edith smoothed the napkin in her lap. "I miss her, too."

Billy nodded, worked his jaw. "Dusty," he said, faltered, began again. "That pain in 'er shoulder . . . 'Twasn't from carryin' dishes, ya know."

She looked up. "No?"

He shook his head. "'Twas somethin' else. That doctor on the island . . .'e was a specialist."

A rustle nearby snapped Edith back to the present, back to the woods. She turned, saw a dark shape moving in the fog. Footfalls sounded, light and stuttery.

"Sonny?" Edith whispered, waited, whispered, "Perdie?"

The shape came nearer. She could see it was four-legged, saw it had a tail; it was an animal, a creature of the night. Terror seized her. A *cougar*? No, she decided: too tall, head too big, tail all wrong. This animal pranced. It whinnied.

"*Pippin?*" Edith gasped.

The horse stopped five yards away, twisted its head side to side, snorted. She extended a hand, palm up, whistled four times, as she'd always done with Pippin. She knew it was lunacy to pretend it could be her horse, but there was an uncanny resemblance. It was the same height. It moved the same, whinnied the same. The horse exhaled, its lips spluttering.

"Pippin," Edith cooed, her voice cracking. "Pippin, it's *me*, Dusty."

She stepped closer. The horse shied, turned as if to bolt.

"No!" Edith said. She couldn't lose her again. "Come, Pippin! *Come!*"

The horse dipped its huge head, heaved it up: a big nod. It turned back around, took a tentative step toward Edith.

"Atta girl," Edith said. "Come on. It's okay."

The horse eased forward; its head emerged from the mist, came into focus. It wasn't Pippin. Edith's sharp intake of breath startled it, and it reared up, whinnied, pawed at the air, blasted its nostrils. Edith shrieked, turned, ran, tripped, scrambled back to her feet, ran. She heard galloping hoofbeats, caught a glimpse of the horse's silhouette ahead in the fog, turned back the way she'd come, ran fast as she could in the mist, fell again, this time into the shrub she had planted. She found herself in a gaping hole in its center, a hole that had not been there before, a hole more than big enough for her to lie in. The soil was disturbed. Roots had been unearthed. Had an animal been at it? There were other holes as well.

The horse neighed sharply, piercingly. It circled her, half hidden in the fog.

"Stop it!" she yelled, then louder, to anyone, "*Help!*"

The hoofbeats slowed, skittered, stopped. The silhouette of the animal grew; it was coming closer. Edith froze. The horse's eyes shimmered. *People love horses for their large, deep eyes*, she recalled her mother saying.

Edith stood up, slowly, silently, barely breathing. The heavy nose nudged her shoulder, blew hot breath onto her neck. She looked up into its face. It was like no horse she had ever seen. Instead of a short, bristly hide, its long face was matted with an olive green carpet of tiny leaves. The eyes were inky, damp, and porous, like wild mushrooms. Webby lichens drooped between stiff, mossy ears: The forelock.

Edith stepped back, wanted to look away, to run away, but couldn't. What she was seeing was impossible. A dream? Was she still in bed, sound asleep? She had to be. *A moss horse?* It didn't feel like a dream, though. It felt real. But wasn't that how dreams always felt? She shut her eyes, willed herself to awaken, pinched herself with what she discovered were fingers so quivery she could barely get them to do her bidding. She opened her eyes. The horse was still there, still green, and a step closer. It nickered and Edith nearly jumped out of her skin. Her stomach heaved. She was going to be sick. Or pass out.

But then the horse flicked its ears. It bowed its head. And Edith, who knew how to read a horse, knew when one was angry, afraid, content, understood that this one was being friendly. She steeled her nerves as best she could, reached out, set her still-trembling hand on the horse's jaw. Its hide was damp. It tickled her palm. It was moss. She jerked her hand back.

"What are . . . ?" she breathed.

The horse's ears rolled forward. Edith moved to its side, reached out again, set her hand on the beast's neck, felt within the moss coat what she assumed to be the strong muscles horses require to hold up such massive heads. But on close inspection, she found instead a tight braiding of woody stems with black, whiskery hairs, each as thick as one of Edith's fingers. The horse was not made of flesh and blood. It wasn't an animal; it was a plant, a living, breathing, galloping, whinnying, horse-shaped plant. A hazel bush—a hazel *horse*.

The black hairs were much the same as those of the shrub. She remembered the hole in the shrub she'd fallen into, the upset soil, the hazel branch, the seeds, the gull . . . her mother. Had Cathy sent Edith this creature? If so, why? To deliver her? To rescue her?

Edith touched the green horse's broad shoulder, estimated its height to be fourteen hands, same as Pippin's. She rubbed its webby mane, its mossy face, cupped a hand under its chin, pursed her lips, puffed into the nostrils. This was how she told Pippin who she was. The horse whickered gently, nodded.

"I'm Dusty," Edith said again.

Suddenly the horse's head shot upright, its ears rolled back, lay flat, its eyes widened.

"What's wrong?" Edith whispered, sensing its alarm.

She heard a crunch, a branch snap, then another. A beam of light sliced through the mist.

"Who's there?" a voice boomed—Book's voice.

The horse spun around, its licheny tail swishing. With one stride it vanished into the fog. Edith listened to its fading hoofbeats. "Don't go," she whispered, pleaded.

She thought to run, too, but knew that would be foolish, and futile.

"It's me, Edith," she called out.

"Edith?"

"Yeah."

The big man emerged from the mist, a grim expression on his face.

"You scream?"

"Yeah," Edith said, trying to act as if nothing incomprehensibly strange had just happened.

He squinted at her. "Why?"

"The horse. It startled me."

Book nodded. "Thought I heard one." He glanced around. "Wonder what a hayburner's doin' out here." He turned his gaze back on Edith. "What're *you* doin' out here?"

Edith shrugged.

"I don't like the sound of girls screaming," Book said, not looking at her, looking above her head, into the fog.

Edith wanted to know what that meant—what girls?—but just answered, "Sorry."

"You're comin' back t' camp with me," he said.

Edith nodded.

As they walked, she kept an eye and ear open for the green horse, but there was no sign of it.

CHAPTER
Five

Edith eased open her drawer, gingerly lifted her mother's hoof-pick out of the tin can. Its diamond eye sparkled in the gloaming. She carried the pick to her bunk, tucked it under her pillow, then slid in under the cool sheets. Her mind, restless before her walk, was now feverish, crazed. She lay awake all night.

Mother Smith's crisp, predawn rap on the door made her jump.

"Get moving, girls," Mother Smith said through

the door. She knocked on the boys' door. "Outta bed, boys."

Perdie stirred in her bunk, moaned, stretched.

"Oh, goody," Hero grouched. "Another day in Camp Nine."

Edith went to the window. The hot sun was burning off the fog. Patches of blue sky peeked through.

Edith dressed, withdrew the pick from beneath her pillow, dropped it into her apron pocket.

"You look jest awful," Perdie said to her on the way to the cookhouse.

"Thanks a lot," Edith said, feeling just awful. "How much do you know about Book?"

"What d'ya wanna know?"

"He told me he doesn't like hearing girls scream."

"Oh, that," Perdie said. "He use' ta have a wife an' daughter livin' with him in a camp where he use' ta work."

"Book was a prune picker?"

"Yup," Perdie said. "An' there was a stove fire one day, an' his wife an' daughter burned up."

"My god!"

"Way I heard it, Book was out in the woods that day, actin' really strange, nervous as a cat, sayin', 'Sump'm's wrong, sump'm's wrong.' Told the bull he could hear his little girl callin' him through the trees. The bull said he was crazy, said it was the wind, wouldn't let him go, but Book run off anyway. Run all the way back to camp, but by then ever'thin' was ashes. That's why he don't like no girls to scream."

Edith's perception of Book turned inside out.

"Ever'body in camp's got some kinda story," Perdie said.

Mother Smith was waiting for them at the cookhouse.

"Edith, I understand you left your room last night," she said, her mouth tight.

Perdie looked at Edith, looked back at Mother Smith. "I didn't see her go out, Mother Smith, ma'am," she said.

"Did you go out, Edith?" Mother Smith said.

There was no point denying it. Book must have told her. "Yes," Edith said.

Mother Smith raised her hand and slapped Edith

across the face. Edith hadn't expected it, caught it flatfooted, staggered backward, her hand feeling for something to support herself. Her vision blurred, her cheek blazed.

"You are *not* to leave the cookhouse today," Mother Smith said sharply. "All your other duties will be given to your sisters. You are not to set a *foot* outside. Do you understand me?"

Edith reeled from the shock of what had just happened. No one had ever done that to her before. "No, ma'am, I certainly do *not* understand you."

Mother Smith slapped her again, on the same cheek, harder. This time Edith was ready, rolled with it.

"You will obey the rules, Edith Smith," Mother Smith said, her voice trembling now. "Or obedience will be beaten into you." She walked away, her boot heels clicking on the plank floor. Over her shoulder, she said, "Mrs. Keckonius, see to it that Edith does not leave the cookhouse today."

"Ain't my job," Mrs. Keckonius said, not looking up from her work. "I'm cook, not babysitter."

The heels stopped. "Leave this room, Edith Smith," Mother Smith said, "an' you will receive the whippin' a' yer life!"

"I just did," Edith said, her jaw set.

Mother Smith fumed. "Perdie," she said, "fetch me a switch."

While Perdie stammered, Edith ran for the door. She burst outside, made her way along the causeways. Tears stung her eyes. A man stepped out of a bunkhouse door. Edith crashed into him.

"Whoa, missy," he said, helping her up.

It was Book. Edith growled at him.

"You again," he said, tobacco juice dribbling over his lower lip.

"You *told*," Edith said, her rasp rising into a screech. "You *told* about last night."

"No, I did not," the logger said.

Edith eyed him. "You d-didn't?"

"No, miss. I mind my own yard." He tipped his hat. "Morning, miss." He went on his way.

"*Hero*," Edith breathed. She could not begin to fathom why Hero could not mind *her* own yard.

"It doesn't matter," she said aloud to herself. She reminded herself the camp was leaving. Sonny was leaving. She was leaving: She had a horse. She ran ahead and didn't look back.

The sun shone brightly as she reached the pitch-fork. A wisp of steam nested in the cedar stump. Edith kneeled by the hazel branch.

"I'm getting out of here," she said to it.

She stood, whistled four times, waited. A crow squawked. A train whistle blew. No hoofbeats. Edith slid her hand into her pocket, gripped the hoof-pick, felt its sharp diamond eye press into her palm. She whistled again. She worried the horse only came out at night, or in the fog. Understandably it didn't want to be seen. She worried that she had dreamed the whole thing. A horse made of moss and vine? Was she mad? It had been late and foggy. Maybe her head had been foggy. No, no, she'd *touched* it. It was strange, frightening, but real.

So where was it? She had flagrantly disobeyed Mother Smith, could not go back, yet couldn't stay where she was. Without a doubt Hero knew about

Edith's place, had followed her there before, would lead Mother Smith to it. She had to keep moving. With luck the horse would find her.

She headed off away from the hazel branch, her mother's marker, away from the shrub that had sprouted from the seeds she'd planted, away from the tracks, toward the hills, toward the woods, away from everything having to do with Camp Nine. Perdie? She'd have to fend for herself. Edith hated being so callous, but she had her own welfare to consider. One teenager was all she could handle. Sonny? He had his own escape planned, his and Jed's both. True, he'd invited her along, but Edith wouldn't allow herself to believe he'd meant it. Even if he had, why should she trust Sonny's father? Why had he abandoned his sons in the first place? If she went with Sonny, she could potentially end up a slave again. But there was more to it than that. Something told her not to put her faith in Sonny, not to hitch her wagon to him. She knew somehow not to hitch her wagon to any man. Had it been her mother who'd said so, or Mae West?

If she was going to trust anyone, it was the green

horse. That sounded crazy to her, but she knew that, like the hazel branch, the gull, the seeds, and the shrub, the horse led somehow back to her mother. Her mother she trusted.

"Here, horse!" she called. "Here, green horse! Come, girl—or boy!"

Once she knew its sex, she told herself, she'd come up with a name—that is, if it had only one sex. It was a plant, after all.

Again she wondered whether she'd only dreamed it.

She continued on, wishing she'd worn dungarees like a logger rather than the knee-length cotton Mother Hubbard of a flunky girl, wishing her legs were protected from the splintery terrain. She mounted a small hill, then another. When she looked back, the only sign of Camp Nine was its smoke. She could still hear the speeder, though, taking the men out to the woods, taking Sonny. The camp would go on without her. She'd be easily replaced. There were plenty of orphans to be had.

When she came at last upon a path, an old skid

road, she practically skipped down it. It led to the untouched forest's edge, which was trimmed neat as a hedge. Edith assumed it to be the limit where, for whatever reason, the company had been forced to stop cutting. Maybe the forest there was on public land, or it was someone's private land. As Edith stood gazing up at the dizzying height of the trees, a piece of the forest shifted position. A shrub *moved*.

"Oh!" Edith squealed. "It's you!"

The horse pranced out of the forest like any horse of flesh and blood would, its chin tucked, feet light, tail high. Seeing it for the first time unobscured by mist or darkness, Edith nearly shrieked. Green moss covered everything that hide normally did. Gossamer lichen flowed from its crest and dock. Sunshine streamed *through* the beast.

Edith held out her hand, clucked her tongue. The creature approached. Edith moved alongside it. With bent fingers, she hooked the horse under the jaw, felt its warm breath, inhaled its salty, mildewy aroma. The lips and nose, so supple on a flesh-and-blood horse, were, like the eyes, slick and spongy. Behind the lips were rows of pointed wooden teeth, top and bottom. A shiny, ink-black tongue lolled within. Edith leaned closer, peeked through the moss at the mesh of stems within, stroked the rippling neck, the sinewy stems so like a horse's rippling muscles, patted the shoulder and rump. She felt the horse's chest rise and fall, spied something dark inside inflating, deflating, inflating. Lungs? She puffed into the large nostrils, said, "I'm Dusty."

She reached down, deftly bent the knee of the near foreleg, lifted the foot, inspected the hoof. It was shaped much like the hoof of its animal counterpart, though made of wood rather than horn, and sheathed in bark. Edith found pebbles, twigs, and other debris wedged between the sole and the frog. She dug the hoof-pick out of her pocket.

"Be steady now," she said, getting to work.

The horse offered no resistance. When Edith finished, she lifted the near hind leg, cleaned its hoof, then the off hind, being extra careful to keep a hand on as she passed around the rump. This was how you kept a horse off your toes, and from kicking. Horses have blind spots both behind and in front of them. A rear kick from a spooked horse can crack a person's rib, or cave in a skull.

"No curry in the world will get through that tail," Edith said.

As she bent down for the last hoof, she peeked beneath the horse. She saw no indication of sex. She did find catkins, which suggested the necessity of pollination: Other such horses would be needed for procreation. Were there others?

When the hooves were all picked clean, Edith smiled. "Well, Hazel," she said, for that was what she chose to call the horse, "what are we waiting for?"

She led Hazel to a stump. "Whoa now," she said as she scaled it. She gripped the dewy mane, slung a leg over, sank into the horse's moist, cushiony back. She felt her dress dampen under her, felt the twining wooden skeleton pressing through the moss, pressing against the inside of her legs. This was only the second time she'd ridden bareback, the first being the night she fled her father. Sitting on Hazel was only a little less comfortable than sitting on Pippin had been.

Edith clucked her tongue, said, "Giddyup," gave Hazel a gentle tap with her heels. The horse took a step, then another. Edith grasped tighter to the mane with one hand, patted the horse's neck with the other. "Attagirl," she said, electing to overlook the fact that she had no idea whether the horse was exclusively female.

She led Hazel in a circle, turning her with pressure, the Western way. She practiced trotting. She taught her to stop when she tugged her mane and called, "Whoa." Hazel was either an apt pupil or had already been trained. When Edith was satisfied that she had some control, she leaned forward, pressed her knees against the horse's belly, goaded her into a canter. Hazel's body creaked like a saddle, like a rocking chair, like the *Stormy Petrel* at sea. Edith rode her up and down the skid road, worrying at first that they'd be spotted (a girl on a green horse!), but reassured herself that the road was out of sight of the camp, and the tracks ran through nothing but ruin. She clucked her tongue, coaxed her mount into a gallop. Hazel was light-footed, agile, accommodating. She absorbed her rider, moved in harmony with her. The air in Edith's face as they flew was the freshest, richest she could remember.

It's so easy to fall in love with a horse, Edith thought. She'd fallen for Pippin instantly, fallen for her strength, her beauty, her grace, her deep eyes and flowing hair. After one ride, Edith and Hazel were wed for life.

But where could she live with such a horse? Somewhere away from people, she told herself. Deep in the forest maybe, deeper than the lumber company ventured. Was there such a place? She toyed with the idea of escaping civilization, becoming a hermit, a savage, a wild woman of the woods. She laughed, imagining what her mother, the princess of pig iron, the cultured lady, would say about that. But hadn't Cathleen done much the same thing when she'd left home? Didn't she trade high society for the high seas? She had challenged herself to live a new way, without the comforts of her parents' world, to find out what she was made of, what she could become. Edith would do the same.

She led Hazel to the forest's edge again, prepared to dive into the wilderness, into her future, but before she was able to, another shrub moved, another horse, one like Hazel.

Edith understood what this meant, what she had to do: She had to find Sonny. She stepped slowly toward the second horse. This one's face was narrower, longer, its mane darker, its knees knobbier, its coat more mottled, but they were of the same species, whatever species that was. The two horses acknowledged each other with nods and whinnies. The new horse, which Edith knew not to name—its rider would do that—fell in behind Hazel, nose to tail.

By now the men would be in the woods, sawing and chopping where they had left off the day before. She was certain they wouldn't be hard to find. She'd follow the din of saws and axes, the screeching of the steam donkey, the crashes of falling trees.

"Giddyup, Hazel," she said.

Hazel found a sliver of a path, carried Edith into

the forest, the other horse close behind. The temperature dropped twenty degrees, from summer to spring. The light shifted from bright to dusky. Everything was green, as if Edith wore tinted eyeglasses, like those Dorothy Gale wore in the Emerald City. The tree trunks were wrapped in velvety green moss, the ground blanketed by enormous green ferns that swiped at Edith's bare legs. They passed moss-covered deadfall, huge moss-covered boulders, moss-covered earth. Hazel looked right at home. Firs and cedars rose so high Edith had to crane her neck back to see their tops. The massive cedars, green boughs drooping, heavy with flattened, scaly leaves, had the same sharp odor of the chest at the foot of her parents' bed, the one that kept Cathleen's fine woolens safe from moths. The more numerous firs bore bare, stumpy arms up to near the very top, over a hundred feet from the forest floor, where longer leaved branches competed for sunlight. The high ceiling, the low underbrush, the spaciousness, the stillness, combined to give Edith the impression of a cathedral. Every breath felt like four.

The trail led deeper into the woods, up hills and down, none of the slopes very steep, none of the valleys flat. There were caves tucked into rocky hillsides, cedars whose trunks were opened at the bottom wide enough for a person to step through, sprawling webs that broke on Hazel's muzzle, caught in Edith's flypaper hair. Sometimes coming around or over a hill, the sound of rushing water would reach her ears, except for some sodden stretches of the path and some tiny, trickling streams, though she and Hazel came upon no river.

Edith was on her own in a way she had never been before, not even after her father had left her alone in the house. At least then there had been help (policemen, doctors, grocers) if she'd really needed them. Even in camp there were people to call on. In the forest there was no one. She had entered a place, like the open sea, that existed beyond mankind, where voices and machines were replaced by the sound of wind and water, where everything seemed to glisten, where magic seemed to dwell, a place of enchantment.

Though the only animals Edith saw were squirrels

and birds, she knew there were others. Sonny spoke of commonly seeing deer, elk, porcupines, bears, and cougars in the woods. Mickey had once described for Edith in detail, and with obvious relish, how a cougar hunts: The great cat stalks its unwitting prey for days, awaiting the ripest opportunity to strike; when it strikes, it does so from behind and above; it lets out a bloodcurdling scream as it springs onto its victim's back, which freezes the hapless creature in its tracks; the beast lands with such tremendous force it slams the prey to the ground; then, with uncanny precision, it plunges its needle-sharp fangs into the victim's nape, piercing vertebrae, puncturing the spinal cord, ending the animal's life deftly and instantly. Once these thoughts entered Edith's mind, they would not be driven out. The forest's stillness took on a new significance. Every cliff, every boulder became a potential panther perch. She wondered if some of the magic she sensed around her was black. Her heartbeat quickened; her head jerked left, right, up, to the rear—especially to the rear—like a chicken's.

The only advice Mickey offered for combating an

attacking cougar, if you were lucky enough to get an opportunity to combat it, was to kick up a fuss: Yell, scream, throw things—though under no circumstances bend to pick anything up. Edith sang loudly. The first song that came to her was one the loggers sang, "Bury Me Under the Weeping Willow." It was not ideal for her state of mind, but had to do till she could think of something cheerier. She sang the chorus, which was all she knew, at the top of her voice, over and over. She felt silly, but ever so slightly safer.

Later she thought of other songs—"All Bound Round with a Woolen String," "Beans, Bacon, and Gravy," "She Is More to Be Pitied than Censured"— and sang them equally as loud, until an earsplitting, earthquaking crash struck her dumb. The horses reared, neighed in fright. Edith climbed down, stroked Hazel, cooed in her ear, knew how upsetting noise was to a horse. She massaged Hazel's ear, her thumb inside it. This had always calmed Pippin.

Before long Edith heard a man's voice cry, "Timber!"

"Whoa," she murmured to Hazel.

There was a creaking, a swishing, then another rumbling crash, a chattering of the birds, a flapping of wings, then another tremor, this one stronger than the first. Again the horses reared.

She calmed them, then whispered, "It's okay. Stay here. I won't be gone long."

CHAPTER
Six

The loggers were cutting a swath through the trees over a nearby crest. In the middle of the wreckage stood a tall, limbless trunk, a network of cables connected to its top, like a telephone pole. Logs were being hoisted high above the ground by the cables, which were being driven by the huge revolving spools of the steam donkey.

Everything Edith knew about logging she had picked up listening to the loggers, especially Sonny. She knew the fallers felled the trees, the buckers cut them into log lengths and stripped the bark, the rigging crew yarded the logs to the cold deck where they were loaded onto a lokie bound for the sawmill. Sonny, as the whistle punk, stood in the middle of it all, worked with the riggers, relaying messages via the steam whistle between the rigging slinger and the donkey engineer.

No part of the process was immune to danger, Sonny said. Logs were unpredictable, whether hurtling through the air or lying in stacks. Piles of them sometimes toppled, flattening any loggers in their path. Trees rarely fell true, sometimes "jumped" or "walked" or collided with other trees, causing a chain reaction: enormous, lethal dominoes. Falling trees hammered men into the ground like nails. Falling limbs, which the loggers called "widow-makers," crushed skulls. Steam donkeys, straining all day under hundreds of pounds of pressure, were prone to explode. As Sonny said, there were hundreds of ways for a logger to die in the woods.

Edith found him under the hurtling, whining cables, staring up at the gargantuan logs sailing by overhead, jerking a trip wire from time to time to trigger the whistle. In his tin pants, suspenders, calked boots, and flannel newsboy cap, he looked like an authentic logger, though, to Edith, he was nothing of the kind. He was just a boy, a nature boy, a lover of trees. Edith crept as close to him as she could without being seen, hid behind a huge fir stump, tried to catch his eye. His attention was too riveted to his work. She decided it was unwise to distract him.

An hour or so later the bull called for lunch. The clamor ceased. The forest sounds returned. Sonny glanced around uneasily, as if sensing someone was watching him. Edith waved when he spotted her. He didn't yell out, understood he was not supposed to. He walked over, mindful of whether anyone was watching.

"Whatcha doin' out here?" he asked. "D'ya come to tell me yer goin' with?"

That threw her. She'd been thinking of saying only one thing: "Come on!" Instead she asked, "When are you leaving?"

"Tomorrow."

"No," she said, her purpose returning. "You're coming with me."

"With you?" Now it was he who was thrown.

Edith knew any explanation would sound preposterous, if not insane. "Come with me," she said. "I . . . *found* . . . something you need to see."

"Now? I can't leave. Leavin' a show's a hangin' offense." He grinned.

"You have to come."

"What d'ya find?"

Again she phrased it carefully so as not to sound wild-eyed. "A way out of here that's better than hopping a train. A lot better." It was her turn to grin.

"Oh, yeah? What?"

"Come with me," she said, tugging at his sleeve. "I'll show you."

"Edith, I can't!" he said, jerking free. "Ya don't go messin' aroun' with loggers, not if you wanna keep on livin'. They're mean an' strong an' they got axes."

Edith scowled. He wasn't taking her seriously.

"Forget about them," she said. "You'll never see any of 'em again."

Sonny squinted. "What about Jed?"

Edith had forgotten about him. "Go and get him. I'll meet you both at the hazel branch. I'll be hiding, so whistle four times."

"Whistle? What're ya talkin' 'bout? Ya gone crazy? Look, I can't jes' walk off a show an' go waltzin' into camp an' drag my brother away. If the loggers don't kill me, Mother Smith sure will."

Edith shut her eyes. Things were getting complicated.

"What's the hurry?" Sonny said. "Why ya way out here anyhow?"

"I ran away," Edith said, opening her eyes. "Mother Smith hit me. I'm not going back."

"She hit ya?" A flush of pique rose in his cheeks.

"It doesn't matter. What matters is something *happened* last night. Something . . . I don't know . . . *big*. Something amazing. But real. They're *real*. And they can take us away from here."

"*Who's* real, Edith? Yer not makin' any sense."

She took a breath. "Horses. Two of them. One for me. One for you and Jed."

"*Horses?* We're gonna ride *horses* to my pa's farm?"

"Why not?"

"It's a long way, that's why not. An' lokies are a lot faster. An' easier."

"Horses are safer. If you get caught hopping a train you'll get tossed in jail, and then sent back to camp."

"We won't get caught."

"Well then, what if you fall trying to climb on? Or klutzy Jed does?"

"Look, I can't talk about this right now. We can discuss it later, after supper."

"I'm not going back," Edith said, getting angry. This was why she had trouble trusting him. He didn't always listen very well. "I ran away, remember?"

"All right, simmer down. Why don't we meet up behind the equipment shed, the one 'cross from our bunkhouse?"

"Why do I have to come into camp? Why can't you just get Jed and meet me out at the hazel tree?"

"I told you, I jes' can't. I gotta think an' I can't think right now. I gotta get down there an' eat my lunch, an' then I gotta finish my shift. I can't walk out.

I may jes' be a punk, but a punk does count fer sump'm out here."

Edith sighed. "All right. I'll meet you."

"Behind the equipment shed," Sonny said, edging to leave.

"Yes. Bring slickers. And food." She hoped he was listening.

He nodded. "Where d'ya find horses anyhow?"

"I didn't find them. They found me."

As she walked away, she second-guessed her decision to seek out Sonny. Why hadn't she even entertained the idea that he might not drop everything for her? Why had she neglected to consider Jed? Had she misinterpreted the appearance of the second horse? Maybe it was meant for someone else. Perdie, maybe. After all, Sonny and Jed had a place to go.

She kept to the path as best she could, but it split, then split again, then again. She couldn't be sure she hadn't taken at least one wrong turn. She tried to retrace her steps, but it was impossible. She told herself she hadn't lost the horses forever, that somehow they'd find her. Then the thought of cougars popped back into her head. Without the horses, she was utterly alone, easy prey. The horses would have sensed trouble when she couldn't. Their quick reflexes and speed would have helped in escaping. And, if necessary, the horses were fully capable of defending themselves, of fighting back, of kicking and screaming.

Edith scurried down the path, belting "Beans, Bacon, and Gravy," disbelieving her situation, cursing it, angry at herself for leaving Hazel for Sonny—ungrateful, mocking Sonny—angry that her mother had gone and died on her. *That* was the reason she was lost in cougar-infested woods. It was the reason for every bad thing that had happened to her.

Then, sauntering up from an intersecting trail, the horses came into view. Edith rushed up and threw her arms around Hazel's neck, sobbed into it.

"Let's stay together from now on," she whispered.

Hazel carried her back through the forest to the skid road, from there to the cedar stump and the hazel branch.

Supper wasn't for hours. To take her mind off

the wait, Edith groomed Hazel. Grooming had always been comforting to her. She handpicked debris out of Hazel's mane, tail, and coat. The other horse stood apart, watching. When she finished with Hazel she held out a hand to it, clucked her tongue. It hung its head, walked toward her. Edith set her palm on its shoulder, looked into its murky eyes, blew into its nostrils, started falling in love all over again.

Her father used to tease her about her love of horses, saying that it was unnatural to spend so much time with them and that she really ought to try human beings, maybe make some friends. Her mother would retort, "Oh, it's so much more natural to worship wooden tubs." The remark was intended to get him to ease up on Edith, to get him to lighten up, but any mention of boats always made him brood instead.

"Love your horse, Dusty," Cathleen told Edith. "She can be counted on."

Edith was happiest when at the stables. If having a horse removed her from the sporting and social events so essential to her peers, Edith certainly did not feel the loss. And she had plenty of friends. Most of them just happened to be horse girls. Horse girls had everything in common, including a language horseless people didn't understand. They knew they were the butt of jokes at school, that they were called names—"tomboy," "shitkicker"—though mostly by dumb boys. Edith believed every girl on earth was dying for a horse, at least on the inside. She'd seen the doodles in the margins of their notebooks. Any taunt from a horseless girl was sour grapes, pure and simple.

Pippin had been a gift from a woman at the stables who'd bought her for fun and exercise, but who rapidly grew weary of the expense of keeping her. Edith continued to call the horse Pippin, for she knew it was bad luck to rename a horse.

Lola Nye became Edith's best friend in fifth grade primarily because Lo got her pony, Raindrop, at about the same time Edith got Pippin. Edith wondered if Lo had found a new best friend yet. If so, probably Mirna Rowley, another horse girl in their circle. Edith had fully intended to write to Lo every day, but could never find the time or energy. She doubted Lo would care to hear about her dreadful life at the camp anyway. Why would she want to listen to sob stories? Sob stories were a dime a dozen these days.

As Edith groomed the second horse, she debated whether or not to start calling it Raindrop. If she did, Sonny couldn't change it, and he needed all the luck he could get. She refrained, decided to leave the joy of christening to him.

When she'd finished grooming the horse, she rode Hazel back to the woods. All her nagging worries, doubts, and fears were erased by the beating hooves, the flowing mane, the straining muscles, the blurring world. So high from the ground, so fast, it was like flying, or as close to it as Edith had ever come. Pippin had always been remarkably responsive, but Hazel anticipated Edith the way her mother had. Cathleen would hand her a napkin before Edith could even say she'd spilled, a sweater before she complained of a chill. Hazel understood her that way as well.

Her hunger couldn't wait till supper. She hadn't eaten all day. Riding did more than help Edith forget her stomach; it helped her forget everything. It had always done that. She found plenty of blackberry bushes, but berries didn't stick to her ribs. Mrs. Keckonius said Indians lived off forest plants, knew which were edible, which poisonous. Edith wished she were an Indian.

The horses turned up their noses at the blackberries. Edith had never seen them graze, never seen them eat or drink. Didn't they need to? They were plants. Maybe all they needed was water and sunshine. Then what were their teeth and tongues for? Vocalizing?

Edith went deeper into the forest in search of food, soon heard the steam donkey again, the saws, falling trees; she felt the earth tremble. Without meaning to, she had ridden back within earshot of the show. Later she heard a whistle and a voice cry, "All in!" Quitting time. The loggers would be heading back to camp. Edith turned Hazel around.

She left the horses at her mother's hazel branch, which she had thought she would never see again, walked back to camp, her heart in her throat. The loggers arrived first, were trudging from the speeder to the cookhouse, some stopping at the equipment sheds to drop off their gear, some at the privies, some at the showers. Edith didn't worry about their seeing her. They wouldn't know she'd run away. She didn't really worry about bumping into Mother Smith either, figuring she'd be too busy in the cookhouse. She did worry, however, about nosy, blabbing Hero.

She hid behind the shed across from her bunkhouse, or rather, what *had* been her bunkhouse. She was tempted to steal in, get some extra clothes, her hairbrush, her tin can, but decided none of it was worth the risk. She had the hoof-pick in her pocket. Everything else was just stuff.

The smell of roast chicken wafted in from the cookhouse. She hoped Sonny would remember to bring food.

"What're you doin' there, princess?" an unctuous voice said. It was the bull, Prescod.

Edith said nothing, sidled away. He followed.

"Where ya goin'?" he said, laughing. "It's me, yer Prince Charmin', 'member?"

Edith ducked behind a privy, heard dreadful sounds emanating from inside, ran off along a causeway, out in the open, around a bunkhouse, and back to the equipment shed. She sat on the ground, took a deep breath, looked down at her big hands. They were shaking.

Sonny showed up half an hour later.

"I bet yer starvin'," he said with a smile.

He held out a napkin. Inside it were fried chicken legs and buttered biscuits. Edith snatched a biscuit, stuffed it in her mouth.

"Got ya a slicker an' a blanket," Sonny said, holding up a bindle. "Put a canteen a' water in there, too."

Edith grunted, started on a chicken leg.

"I ain't told Jed yet," he said.

Edith stopped chewing. "Why not?"

"Ain't had a chance. He's in the cookhouse washin' dishes."

"So when are you going to tell him?"

"Later. Don' worry. He'll do whatever I say."

"I thought we'd be leaving right away."

"I told ya I needed to think about it."

"You had all afternoon."

"I was kinda busy, Edith."

"Well, I'm leaving tonight." She sighed. "With or without you."

"That don't make sense."

"Why not?"

"Ya gonna ride all night?"

Edith shrugged. "I don't mind." She finished the leg, took another.

"Well, I can't stay up all night. I'm bushed. Imagine Jed is, too."

"Where am I going to sleep?" Edith said, not relishing the thought of traveling all night alone.

"It's a warm night. You got a blanket. Camp out." Edith studied him closely. "What's the look for?"

"I'm trying to see what you're made of."

He laughed, withdrew another napkin from his jacket pocket, opened it to reveal a slice of apple pie.

"Sugar an' spice an' ever'thin' nice," he said. "So, when you gonna show me these horses of yers?"

A light, sunny rain fell as Edith led him away from camp. A rainbow arced over the mountaintops in the distance.

"Still think I can camp out?" Edith said.

"You ain't sugar."

"No, *you* are."

Sonny laughed.

"Any word on when the camp's pulling out?" Edith asked.

"Prob'ly a week or so."

"Wish we could bring Perdie with us."

"Doubt my pa'd be too happy 'bout *that*."

"I said 'I wish.'"

"Next you'll be wantin' to bring Mickey. An' Hero."

"Mickey'd never leave Mother Smith. But Hero, she'd follow you anywhere."

Sonny smirked. "I think she'd leave with any fella."

"Poor Hero," Edith said.

"Poor *Hero*? You kiddin'?"

"It's no wonder she's so mean. Look at the hand she was dealt. Her father gets killed, her mother dies, then she has to live under Mother Smith's thumb her whole life."

"Her mother din't die."

Edith looked at him. "Perdie said she did."

"Her pa did, but her ma went and took up with another logger. This fella din't like havin' a kid around, so she left Hero with Mother Smith, an' the two of 'em set off."

"Does Hero know that?"

"She's gotta."

Edith revised her opinion of why Hero never talked about the past.

"Where do you think Perdie heard her version?" she asked.

"From Mother Smith, prob'ly. She's always sweetenin' these things up. She don't like things sordid. Y'know, *sinful*."

"Like a mother abandoning her child?"

"Well, the loggers say Hero's ma wudn't sure exactly who Hero's pa really was. She claimed it was the foreman. Foreman gets the most pay, if you get my meanin'."

"You saying Hero's mother—"

"I ain't saying nuthin' but what I heard."

Edith pondered this a moment, then asked, "What's Mother Smith say about my parents?"

"That they drowned at sea. That right?"

For the first time, Edith had a tender thought for Mother Smith.

"That's right."

"I guess Mother Smith din't need to sweeten it."

"Guess not."

"Sorry 'bout yer folks."

Edith nodded. "I feel kinda sorry for Mother Smith."

"First Hero, now Mother Smith! You crackin' up on me?"

"Father Smith leaves her to run the place most of the time. No wonder she's so cross. She must be lonely."

Sonny sniggered.

"What?" Edith said.

"Nuthin'." He sniggered again.

"Tell me."

"It's just that I don't think she's been too lonely."

"What do you mean?"

"Well, she takes . . . visitors."

"Visitors? You mean *men*?"

Sonny grinned, cocked an eyebrow.

"Who?"

"The loggers say it's the bull."

"*Prescod?* But he's so disgusting."

Sonny shrugged. "Beauty's in the eye a' the beholder."

"It must be," Edith said.

When they reached the cedar stump, Edith whistled for the horses. After one look at Hazel, Sonny fainted dead away. Edith struggled to keep him from hurting himself as he fell, but he was heavy and pulled them both down. When he revived, he found himself lying with his head in her lap. He sat up with a jerk. The horses were standing over them.

"Wh-what are they?" he said.

"Friendly," Edith said.

She explained about the gull, the seeds, the shrub. It sounded crazy, she said, but they had no choice but to accept it. The proof was snuffling at his trouser leg.

He stood up, looked closely at Hazel. "It's covered with *moss*."

"The mane's lichens, I think," Edith said, then laughed. "Horsehair lichen, in fact. That's its real name!"

"It's breathin'."

"She," Edith said. "Though, I think they have both—"

She let that drop.

"I call her Hazel. The other one's yours to name."

Sonny looked at the other horse, walked up to it, stroked it.

"I'll call him Mossy."

So much for Raindrop, Edith thought. "Him, huh?"

"Yup."

"Do you ride?"

"Nope."

"I'll teach you."

First she taught him to mount: where to hold, how tightly, how to distribute his weight. He was agile, had good balance, learned fast, liked showing off, was thrown a few times because of it. He soon wearied of trotting, goaded Mossy into a canter, wanted to go faster still, to gallop, to fly. Edith followed him on Hazel.

"Patience, jack. You can't have everything at once."

"Why not?" Sonny said with a wink.

The rain picked up, the drops spattering on the horses' moss, on Edith's and Sonny's slickers, into their open mouths. Edith laughed so much her ribs ached.

"This way!" Sonny yelled, when the rain became too much.

She followed him along the tracks, away from the camp, to a small shack. The door was off its hinges, its windowpanes broken, its paint peeling. Edith and Sonny hopped down from Hazel and Mossy, dashed inside. The roof leaked. Edith shivered. Sonny wrapped his arm around her. She folded into him. He rubbed her arm through her slicker. He put his other arm around her, hugged her close, their cheeks pressed together. They were almost exactly the same height.

"It's cold," she said.

"Summer's endin'," he said.

"How'd you know about this place?"

"Been by it on the speeder, when we was workin' out this way."

"I could sleep here tonight," she said, then pulled back. "In the shack, I mean."

He stared at her. It scared her.

"You should get back before they miss you."

"I will," he said, but she could tell he didn't want to.

"You should go *now*. We don't want Mother Smith suspicious. We're leaving in the morning, right?"

Sonny sighed heavily. "Yeah. Before wake-up. I'll try to get Jed up, try to swipe some food."

"Don't *try* to get him up—get him up."

"You took me by surprise last night," Sonny said. He grinned slightly, looked down, seemed embarrassed.

Edith winced, comforted herself that he'd been as clumsy as she, hoped it had been his first kiss as well. He was sixteen, but there were no girls in camp but his "sisters." Edith shuddered: Had he ever kissed Hero?

Before she could rid herself of this terrible thought, he kissed her. This time their lips matched up fine. Edith set an open palm against his chest, pushed herself away from him.

"Scram, jack," she said.

Sonny smiled, laughed, neither convincingly. "Okay. Got your bindle?"

"Got it."

He tied his hood. "I'll be back before dawn." He ran outside. The rain pounded on his slicker. He turned back.

"Hey!" he yelled.

Edith peered out. There were five dark horse-shaped silhouettes where there had been two.

CHAPTER
Seven

Rain fell all night. Edith hunkered in the driest corner of the shack, the one with only an inch of standing water. Water seeped in through the cracks in her galoshes. She wondered whether she'd ever be able to straighten up again. Sleep came in fits.

Her heart went out to those poor people back in the hobo jungles. Was this how it started? A night comes when you find you don't have a place to live anymore, so you sleep where you can, slap together a shelter with whatever materials you have at hand. It hit Edith that she was homeless, penniless, a waif, an urchin, a hobo, a bum. How could things change so much, so fast? Only last fall . . .

That kind of thinking led nowhere. She was what she was, where she was: A runaway orphan hiding in a leaky shack in a rainstorm, in the wilderness, destitute, adrift, alone. She'd thought she'd hit bottom after her mother died, then again after her father abandoned her. But at least then she'd had a home.

Edith spent the month after her father left waiting for the door to open, for him to return, or her mother to. Surely she couldn't have lost them both. Footsteps on the walk outside—the postman, a passerby—caused her heart to miss a beat. She hid from all those who knocked, who phoned, even her best friend, Lo. She ceased using electricity, collected water in a rain barrel, rationed what little food remained in the pantry and the garden. She wanted the world to think she was not there alone, that she and her father had gone away together, sailed away somewhere on the ketch, to forget, to start over. She especially feared being discovered by the relief, the people who took orphans away and placed them in new homes, as if they were furniture.

Edith considered taking it on the lam with Emma and Pippin, but she was too practical to see running away as a solution. That was her father's way: When things get hard, pack up and sail away. Besides, where could she run? Would things be any better someplace else?

Edith didn't run away; though, in hindsight she wished she had, for a woman knocked on the door one day, let herself in when no one answered, found Edith hiding in the stables. She identified herself as a social worker, asked Edith where her parents were.

"I can't say," Edith said.

"You can't say, or won't?" the woman said.

"Can't," Edith said.

The woman took her into custody. When a perfunctory search for next of kin came up empty, she was made a ward of the state. Father Smith showed up, filled out the paperwork, became her legal guardian. When Edith arrived in Camp Nine that night, Mother Smith's first words were, "Till you're ready to return to God, this is where you'll be."

Edith wasn't going to make the same mistake again. This time she would take matters into her own hands, mount her pony, ride away. Where? Anyplace. Even the hobo jungles would be an improvement over Camp Nine. She would never again be anyone's slave.

Nevertheless, as she squatted and sobbed there in that cold, soggy hut, she wondered a thousand times whether she ought to turn back.

Rain still fell as day broke. The sun hid behind a heavy gray sky. Edith found the five horses huddled together, awake, their heads nodding, nostrils blasting out water. "Hello there," she cooed, stepping stiff-leggedly out of the shack, hobbling from one horse to another, stroking them, blowing into their nostrils, falling head over heels. One taller than both Hazel and Mossy, with larger, darker eyes, a dappled coat, an aquamarine mane and tail. Another, the shortest, was lean and lively with a deep blue-green hide and pea-green hair. The last was barrel-chested, slow-moving, calm as an old mare. Its coat was the color of cabbage, its long, flowing tail a darker shade of it.

Hazel. Mossy. One for Jed. One for Perdie. The last for Hero. Much as she would have liked to, Edith could not leave Hero behind. She knew only too well how that felt.

There was no horse for Mickey, which Edith took to mean he was not to be included in the escape. It saddened her to think Mickey could be so beholden to Mother Smith that he wouldn't jump at the chance to flee, but put it down to his never having known anything else. Not only would he not be invited, he would not even be informed of the plan; he was too likely to rat them out.

Feeling conspicuous standing with five mossy horses by the side of the tracks, Edith led them away, hid them behind a giant, fallen redwood. The others soon appeared, shiny in their hooded black slickers, sloshing in their matching galoshes through the mire the night's rain had made of the exposed ground.

Sonny carried his fiddle case and his bindle, which was filled to bursting. Jed and Hero trudged along behind. Edith scaled the redwood trunk, stood atop it.

"Where's Perdie?" she yelled.

"Gone," Sonny answered.

"*Gone?*" Edith jumped down, ran to them. "Gone *where?*"

Sonny pulled off his hood. "She took off yesterday, after you did. No one told me 'bout it till I got back last night."

"She left a note sayin' she was goin' to try to find her crazy mama, an' for nobody to come after her," Hero said wearily, as if it put her out to have to discuss the matter.

"She'll never make it on her own!" Edith said. "Did she take a train?"

"She's stupid," Hero said, "but she ain't stupid enough to try an' make it on foot. It's over a hunnert miles. But she is crazy, jes' like her mama."

Sonny had asked Edith the night before how he was supposed to convince Hero to come.

"Just ask her," Edith had replied.

It had worked. She had come. Now Edith wondered why she'd wanted her to.

"I'm hungry," Jed whined.

"Did you bring food?" Edith asked Sonny.

"What I could."

"They'll come after us, y'know," Hero said. "Mother Smith'll call up the other camps an' tell 'em to be on the lookout for some damn fool runaways. Then they'll drag us all back an' whip us within an inch a' our lives."

"I doubt that," Sonny said. "Who's she gonna get to come after us? The loggers'd never do it. Father Smith's away. She'll prob'ly figure we won't get far 'fore we get hungry or scairt an' turn back."

"Which we will," Hero said.

"You can go back right now, Hero," Edith said. "No skin off my nose."

"I'll take some skin off your nose," Hero snarled.

"Look!" Jed said, pointing.

Hazel had stepped out from behind the log. The others were edging out behind her.

"Jeepers!" Jed said. "Horses! Which one's mine?"

"The short one," Edith said.

He raced toward it. "My own horse! I can't believe—" He froze in his tracks. "Hey! What kinda—"

Hero pulled off her hood, moved a few steps closer, stopped. "What are they . . . wearing?"

"They're *green*," Jed said.

Edith exchanged knowing glances with Sonny, then explained. Jed was amazed, but had no trouble believing every word. He rushed up to his horse, ran his hand over its hide.

"It's *soggy*," he said, both disgusted and delighted.

"I ain't riding on no *bush*," Hero said. She affected nonchalance, but a tremble in her voice gave her away.

"I will!" Jed said. "Can I ride him, Sonny?"

"Him?" Edith said.

Sonny laughed. "It's up to Edith. She's the horse expert 'round here."

"What makes her so expert?" Hero said.

"She can ride," Sonny said.

"Then let her. You won't catch me dead on one a' those things."

"What *could* I catch you dead on?" Edith said.

Jed called his horse Champ. Hero reluctantly chose the tall dappled one with the aquamarine mane and tail, but refused to name it. The fifth horse, the one that reminded Edith of an old mare, the one she imagined was Perdie's, remained riderless.

They led the horses away from the track, out of sight, then Edith set about training the flunkies in equitation. She did so in as much haste as she could, for she was anxious to begin hunting for Perdie. Like his brother, Jed was an enthusiastic, impatient student. Unlike Sonny, he was clumsy. To make matters worse, Champ turned out to be a rearer. Jed stuck it out, though, determined to "break" the horse, cowboy style.

"I think he's breaking you," Edith said. "You need to learn to fall, Jed." Her mother taught her early on that falling well was essential to riding well.

"No one gets learnt to *fall*," Jed scoffed.

"Fall wrong and you'll break your neck," Edith said.

"Do what she says, Jedidiah," Sonny said.

Jed fumed, grumbled, sulked, but acquiesced.

Hero wouldn't take a word of instruction from Edith, but eavesdropped during Jed's lessons. Fortunately, Hero's horse was mild-mannered and tolerated her inexperience. Edith secretly enjoyed watching her struggle.

"That's enough lessons," she said. "Let's get goin'. We've got to find Perdie."

Edith agreed they had basic skills enough to trot down a trail. They didn't need to learn to ride well. Riding well took a lifetime. Besides, their mounts were not ordinary horses. If anything, the horses were training their riders. Even Champ seemed to understand the best way to teach Jed was to be a bronco in need of busting, to let Jed think he was in charge.

"Which way do we go?" Edith asked.

"You don't *know*?" Hero said.

Edith stared down her challenge.

"Let's follow the tracks," Sonny said. "They'll lead us in the right direction."

"Okay," Edith said, "but from a distance. We need to stay out of sight." How they could hide a caravan of green horses, she did not know.

"I shoulda stayed in bed," Hero whined.

"It isn't too late to go back," Edith said.

"Giddyup!" Jed said, goading Champ forward with his heels.

"Keep him at a walk, Jed," Edith said. "We're in a hurry, but I don't want to have to stop to nurse your broken neck."

He turned to complain, lost his balance, caught himself. Champ slowed down.

The rest fell in line: Edith on Hazel, Sonny on Mossy, Hero on her nameless horse, and the rider-less one in the rear. The horses' coats were like wet sponges, which made staying aboard arduous. The hard rain kept the riders hunched inside their slickers, kept conversation to a minimum, as they drew nearer to the forested slopes ahead.

After a while, Edith noticed that Hero was lagging behind, that she sometimes stopped her horse, leaned her head out and looked down, as if puzzled by something on the ground. Once when Edith peeked back, Hero was off the horse and sprawled on her belly over a big log. Edith turned Hazel around, rode back to her.

"You okay?" she asked, getting down from Hazel, approaching Hero, setting her hand on her back. Hero pulled away, stumbled off. Edith caught up to her, hooked her arm around her, braced her. She saw and smelled that Hero had been vomiting.

"You sick?" Edith asked.

"Go to hell," Hero spat. She shoved her away, then tripped over an exposed root.

Edith helped her up, peeked inside her hood. Her face was white. Hero pushed her away again, puked again.

Edith, not knowing what else to do, patted Hero's back through her slicker. She heard her mumbling something, could make out only one word: Father. Edith looked ahead to Sonny, saw he had stopped and was reining Jed in. When she looked back, Hero cuffed her across the head, knocking her to the ground. Hero then stood and wobbled off toward her horse. Edith, her ear ringing, chased after her. "You ornery, miserable brat!" Edith snapped. "Can't you tell I'm trying to help you?" She grabbed Hero's arm, hoisted her like a drunken sailor. Hero didn't fight this time. Edith helped her onto her horse.

"I've heard of seasickness," she said, "but never *horse*sickness."

"It ain't the horse," Hero growled.

"Then what?"

Edith couldn't recall Hero coughing or sneezing of late, and Hero was not one to conceal illness. On the contrary, she always broadcast it, milked it, invented it if necessary. Why conceal it now? Did she understand that, away from camp, it wouldn't benefit her, wouldn't get her out of chores, that it might even be viewed as a sign of weakness?

Hero sneered, verged on answering, then said, "Giddyup!"

The horse lurched ahead.

As they traveled on, Edith kept a pace behind Hero, who swayed woozily on her horse. The horses halted at the edge of a forest that was also shorn to some line on some map.

"Come on," Edith said, and clucked her tongue. Hazel walked ahead, located a path. Edith called over her shoulder, "This way!"

One by one they followed her into the woods. The canopy caught much of the rain, funneling it down the long, mossy trunks to the forest floor.

Jed leaned back, silenced a moment by what he saw, then said, "Are there Injuns in here? We ain't got no weapons."

"Prob'ly," Sonny said. "The way the trail meanders, I'd say it was made by Injuns. Loggers cut their trails straight."

"Could be a deer path," Edith said.

"How 'bout cougars?" Jed said.

"We'll be fine," Edith said, not wishing to dwell on that, but secretly worrying more than ever about Perdie. "Just stay together."

The path crossed many other paths. As before, Edith relied on Hazel to lead the way. She couldn't tell how closely they were hewing to the railroad tracks, as it was now obscured by the forest. She heard the sound of a train going by once, but couldn't decide from which direction it was coming.

There was little talk among the riders beyond Jed's occasional "Look at the size of that one!" or "Holy cow!" The forest had overwhelmed them, as it had Edith on her first ride in it. The stillness was ageless. Edith saw it as a prehistoric world, the world as it was before man shuffled onstage with his axes and trains and cities. Had the city she'd grown up in been like this once? The idea seemed preposterous, but, of course, she knew the answer was yes. And there was no reason to doubt that this forest might one day be a noisy, bustling city as well.

Hero leaned over to heave from time to time, but in vain: Her stomach was empty. Soon Jed began to complain that his was, too.

"When do we eat?" he said.

"Blecch," Hero said.

Edith agreed to stop for lunch, but only if it were done quickly.

They stopped when they came upon a large, flat

boulder uncovered by moss. The sun streaked down on it through the trees at a sharp angle, causing steam from the damp needle litter to rise up around it. They dismounted and climbed atop the rock. The horses stood in a tight group, not budging so much as a hoof.

Sonny dumped out the food he'd swiped from the cookhouse: salt pork, cheese, cans of condensed milk, beans, coffee, peaches in syrup, a tin of oats, two loaves of bread, some sugar, carrots, potatoes, a cabbage. He'd also taken a church key, a small cooking pot, some spoons and knives, tin mugs, tin plates, and a box of matches. With his jackknife he began slicing cheese, salt pork, and bread. Edith assembled sandwiches, gave Jed the first one. Hero waved hers away.

"Want coffee?" Sonny asked Edith.

First her father, then Mother Smith had forbidden her to drink coffee, saying it would stunt her growth. Considering how tall she already was, Edith couldn't see how that would be a bad thing.

"Sure," she said.

Sonny went off in search of firewood.

"What's that smell?" said Hero, perched on the boulder, her nose wrinkled exaggeratedly.

Everyone sniffed.

"Polecat," Jed said.

"Disgusting," Hero said.

Sonny returned with chunks and slivers of wood. "Dry wood ain't easy to come by," he said.

He started a fire, poured water from his canteen into the pot, spooned in ground coffee. When it boiled, he poured it through a sock.

"That's how the loggers do it." He poured Edith a mug. "Better have some sugar." He spooned some in for her.

Edith took the mug, stirred the coffee, sipped, hid her reaction to its bitterness.

"Little more sugar?" Sonny asked.

"No, it's fine. Thanks."

"Milk?"

Edith shook her head, now feeling as if she were five again, playing tea party with Mommy, feeling both less and more grown-up.

"I'll take some," Hero piped up. "Black."

"You sure?" Sonny said. "You look kinda green around the gills."

"Just pour."

Sonny filled her a mug. She sipped. She smiled.

Everyone but Hero ate sandwiches. Edith finished her coffee, had another cup, this time with more sugar and a dollop of condensed milk. The back of her eyeballs tingled.

"Nuthin' like drinkin' coffee in the woods," Sonny said.

"I like it better indoors," Hero griped.

Sonny smiled at Edith. She smiled back. Edith blushed, tried to conceal it with her big hands. It was one of those moments when she liked him most, when he appeared to be reading her mind, or her feelings. The smile said, "I'm with you."

When they had been back on the trail a while, Hero said, "I think we been goin' in circles."

"Back there's the sun," Sonny said, pointing over his shoulder, "which means we're headin' east."

"Maybe *now* we are."

"You want to lead the way?" Edith asked.

Hero didn't answer.

"Wait a minute," Edith said, pulling Hazel up short. She looked back. "Where's the other horse?"

"What horse?" Jed said.

"The extra one," Edith said.

Everyone looked around.

"How long has she been gone?" Edith asked.

"What diff—" Hero began to say.

"There!" Edith interrupted, pointing at a piece of shifting vegetation a short distance away. She whistled for the horse. It remained where it was.

"C'mon, Hazel," Edith said, turning her horse around, squeezing past the others. "Let's get 'er."

"We got plenty a' horses," Hero groaned as Edith rode by her. "What we don't got is a way *outta* here."

Edith retraced their steps to the last fork in the trail, took the path they hadn't. It led her to the riderless horse, which was standing beside an old cedar tree, whinnying loudly.

"It's all right," Edith cooed. "It's me, Dusty."

"E-Edith?" squeaked a frail voice. It came from inside the tree.

Edith peered into a large cavity in the trunk. Cowering inside was Perdie.

"Oh, my!" Edith said, overjoyed. "A wood nymph!"

Perdie grimaced, stammered, "N-No, it's m-me, *Perdie*."

Edith laughed, pulled her out. Her hair was filthy and tangled with webs, her Mother Hubbard ripped at the shoulder, her arms and legs cut and bruised. She trembled like a leaf. Edith recalled Perdie saying she thought forests were spooky.

"So what are you doing in a tree, Perdie, dear?" she asked.

"I . . ." Perdie started, then wrapped her arms around herself. Her teeth were chattering. "I h-h-heard s-sump'm." She squinted up at the horses.

"You heard us," Edith said, throwing her skinny arms around Perdie's skinny frame. "And the horses."

"H-horses?"

"Don't worry. They're friendly. I'll tell you about them later," Edith said. "Is this all you wore? No slicker, no galoshes? Did you at least bring any food?"

Perdie shook her head. "Nope. I'm so stupid."

"You're not stupid," Edith said, pulling off her slicker, hanging it on Perdie. "Well, come on. Up we go."

"Up?" Perdie said.

"Onto the horse. She's yours, y'know."

"Mine?"

Edith laughed. "You wished for her, remember?"

Perdie smiled. "Do I get to name 'er?"

"Yes, you do."

Perdie thought a minute. "Princess." She smiled. "How's that?"

"Perfect."

Edith ignored Hero's protests against staying awhile to allow Perdie to eat. While she did, Edith filled her in on what she'd missed: The escape, the horses, their destination.

"Is it okay with Sonny's pa that we're comin' to live with him?" Perdie asked.

"We don't know," Edith said.

"Don't he know we're comin'?"

Edith shook her head.

"What if he don't want us?"

"We'll go someplace else."

"You an' me?"

"Yes."

"What about Hero?"

"Hero can do as she likes."

Perdie sneezed, sneezed again, then again. Her eyes were red and puffy.

"Do you have hay fever?" Edith asked.

"Not that I know of," Perdie answered, sneezing twice more in quick succession.

"You've never been around so much greenery," Edith said.

Perdie looked up at Princess, standing nearby. A yellow butterfly was perched on her ear, waving its wings.

"What about her?" Perdie asked.

"What do you mean?"

"We can't bring *her* to Sonny's farm. Can't let people *see* her."

"No." Edith had thought the same thing many times, had never settled in her mind what to do about it.

"Wherever we end up, I want Princess with me always, ever' minute," Perdie said. "I love 'er. She found me, y'know."

Edith nodded. She had said practically the same words the day she got Pippin.

"She come from *seed*?"

"Looks that way."

Perdie shook her head in disbelief. "I'm never leavin' her. Never."

Edith gave Perdie some quick riding pointers, promised more later, then the five runaways hit the trail, Hazel in the lead.

"Is there cougars 'round here?" Perdie asked.

"You bet there is," Jed said with glee. "Plenty of 'em, just waitin' to pounce."

Edith glared at him, said to Perdie, "Nothing's going to bother us."

"Jes' don't wander off alone," Jed said. "Cougars love to gobble up girls in partic'lar." He smacked his lips.

Edith slid down off Hazel, grabbed Jed by his dungarees, pulled him off his horse.

"Somethin' wrong with your hearin', son?" she said, then boxed his ears.

Jed yelped in pain. "You leave me alone!" he said, trying to wriggle free. But Edith held on.

"I don't want to hear any more about cougars," she said. "Understand?"

"Who d'ya think ya are?" Jed whined.

"Sounds like Mrs. Keckonius to me," Sonny said.

Edith puffed up with pride.

"Jed's right about one thing, though, Edith," Sonny said. "Don't nobody wander off alone. The loggers say cougars don't come 'round if folks stay in bunches."

Jed stuck his tongue out at Edith. She released him.

"Then we'll stay together," Edith said, glaring at him. "We do that and there is *nothing* to worry about, Perdie."

As they pressed on through the woods, Perdie kept imagining cougars' faces in the gnarled bark, their tails in unearthed roots, their ears twitching behind ferns.

"Princess would never let any harm come to us," Edith assured her.

Perdie nodded, but gnawed her lip so much it bled.

The sun was sinking behind them.

"It's getting late," Edith said.

"See," Sonny said, with a look to Hero. "We're headin' east."

"I'm hungry," said Jed.

"What a shock," Hero said.

"Let's find a spot to pitch camp," Edith said.

The sound of rushing water met them as they topped a hill. On the descent, the ground grew soggier and pebblier. At the top of the next hill was a rocky cliff overlooking a raging river. Its roar spooked the horses. Edith jumped down, walked Hazel away, rubbed her ear, instructed the others to do the same.

"This is as good a spot as any," Sonny said.

A fire was kindled, sandwiches made, beans cooked, coffee brewed. They ate by the river. Edith ached all over. She'd lost her riding muscles, her saddle blisters.

"My butt hurts," Jed said.

"Join the club," said Hero.

The aroma the coffee, as well as the tingle drinking it gave, helped ease Edith's discomfort. The warm mug soothed her sore fingers. Gripping Hazel's mane all day had taken its toll. She watched the silver water below surging between stone banks, watched it leap, plunge, crash, eddy, pool. The sky was visible again, a wide, blue stripe dotted between the tree lines. Edith could not deny how pleasant the setting was, could not deny she felt a kind of contentment. She wished she could can the feeling, like baked beans, release them with a church key whenever she needed them.

Jed finished eating first, then searched for a way down to the river. He scooted sideways along a narrow ledge, slipped out of view. Sonny got out his fiddle, scratched out a jig over the rumpus of the river. Hero, sick and sore, did not dance. Jed returned later, said he'd found some caves. Edith and Sonny went with him to investigate, came back with a report that there were indeed three tiny caves in the bluff beneath. Naturally, the caves were damp and cold.

"They'll still be warmer an' drier than sleepin' outside," Sonny said. "Specially if it rains."

Edith led Perdie down, clutching the back of her dress as she sidled along the ledge. Hero groused, but followed. The caves looked out over a small pool created by a bend in the river. Its surface was smooth despite the white water coursing beside it. The bluff muffled the water's sound.

It was decided Sonny and Jed would sleep in one cave, Edith and Perdie in another, and Hero, who refused to share, in the third by herself. Jed threw stones and sticks into the river until he could no longer stay awake. Edith and Sonny whispered conspiratorially about sneaking out after everyone had gone to sleep, then Edith snuggled in with Perdie under Edith's slicker and blanket. To distract Perdie from her worries, she told her a story of a brave giant girl named Polly Bunyan, who towered over the trees, feared nothing, had a pet cougar, drank lakes in a single gulp, used a tree for a fork, and lived happily ever after in the woods. As Perdie was nodding off, Edith tried inching away from her.

"Where ya goin'?" Perdie said suddenly.

Edith sighed. "Nowhere." She settled back in.

Later, with Perdie snoring beside her, Edith heard voices outside.

"Couldn't sleep," Hero said. "It's freezin' in there by myself."

She's practically inviting him in, Edith thought.

"Why don't you crawl in with Edith an' Perdie?" Sonny asked.

That a boy, Edith thought.

"Gee, no thanks," Hero said. "Wanna walk?"

"Uh . . ." Sonny said. He poked his head into Edith's cave, whispered, "You comin'?"

Edith tried to get up but was too entwined with Perdie.

"Can't," Edith answered.

"Darn."

"I'll see you in the morning, I guess."

"Yeah," Sonny said. "'Night."

Edith waited, hoping she'd hear him say the same

to Hero and go back to his cave. When he didn't, she closed her eyes, tried to fall asleep. Images of the romantic scene unfolding on the bluff above in the moonlight, however, kept her awake. She waited to hear them go back to their caves, separately. She fell asleep waiting.

CHAPTER
Eight

Edith woke before Perdie the next morning, slipped out into the mist that clung to the river, peered into the boys' cave, counted four galoshes sticking out from beneath their blankets and slickers, breathed a sigh. She didn't check Hero's cave, didn't want to be caught doing so. What had happened between Sonny and Hero during the night before he returned to his cave, Edith couldn't know, though she felt confident guessing. She knew what Hero was after, was less sure how capable Sonny was to resist it.

She put the question out of her mind by turning her attention to the horses. She climbed up the ledge and found the five of them standing in what appeared to be the same spots as she'd left them the night before, not a hoof out of place.

"Good morning, Hazel," she said, blowing into the horse's nostrils.

The horse nuzzled her hand, licked it with its spongy black tongue.

"What's this?" she said, spying small green buds sprouting from the vining branches within. She fingered one, gently peeled back a sepal, discovered red petals inside.

"Do you flower?"

Hazel dipped her muzzle low, softly fluttered her lips.

"I'll take that for a yes," Edith said, smiling. She massaged the horse's shoulder with the heel of her hand, something Pippin always liked. Edith was growing accustomed to the cold, damp moss, to not feeling Pippin's warm, bristly hide.

"When do you eat?" she asked. "*Do* you eat? Or drink? I've never seen you."

"Me neither," came Sonny's voice from behind her. Edith started, but did not turn around.

"They're plants, though," Sonny said. "Maybe they get their food from the dirt. Do they have roots?"

"How could they walk if they had roots?" Edith said tersely, still not turning around, afraid of what she'd see in his eyes.

"What's the matter?" Sonny said. "Get up on the wrong side of the cave this mornin'?"

Edith said nothing, not wanting to let on what she was feeling, wanting to keep important things from him—the buds, for example.

"I didn't sleep much myself," Sonny said.

Edith flinched, tried to hide it by pretending to brush away a gnat from Hazel's face.

"Jed kep' me up frettin' over cougars," Sonny said.

"Oh," Edith said, a little relieved.

"I'll get a fire goin'," Sonny said.

"I'll do the coffee this time," Edith said. "Yours is too weak."

Sonny chuckled. He really was too likable for his own good, Edith thought.

The first words out of Jed's mouth when he emerged from his cave were. "When's breakfast?"

"Sonny's collecting wood," Edith said. "Why don't you go help him?"

Jed grumbled, trudged away.

By the time Perdie joined the group, the fire was blazing. Her nose was rubbed raw and running. She had sneezed throughout the night, a fact not lost on Edith.

Last to emerge was Hero.

"G'mornin', ever'one!" Hero said in a cheerful voice as she squeezed between the brothers. Her color had returned. Edith couldn't help marveling at her hands, so lithe, so petite, so unlike her own. Her eyes were almost too clear and blue to look at. It would be impossible, Edith thought, even in Hero's unkempt state for anyone, including Sonny, not to find her fair.

"What's fer breakfast?" she said, peeking at Sonny's plate. "Bread an' beans? I am *starved*."

She scooped some beans out onto a plate, shoveled them into her mouth like a logger.

"Want some coffee?" Edith asked, pretending there was nothing upsetting her.

Hero, grinning like a cat with a canary in its mouth, said sweetly, "If it's no trouble, Sister Edith."

"The pleasure's all mine, Sister Hero," Edith said, filling a mug, handing it to her.

"Much obliged," Hero said, lifted the mug to her mouth, sniffed, winced, veiled it with a fake smile, set the mug down.

"Too strong?" Edith asked.

"No," Hero said. "Jest awful smellin'."

Edith glanced at Sonny sipping from his mug. He stared at the campfire.

"So how do we get across the river?" Hero asked.

"Maybe we don't," Edith said. "Maybe we follow it. My guess is it ends up at the sea."

Sonny nodded. "You might be right."

Hero beamed at him, batted her eyelids. "Let's hope she is."

Sonny squirmed, his eyes still trained on the fire.

So that was how it was, Edith thought. She and Hero were competing for the same boy. Why did that bother her so? Was she in love? Was that why she didn't sleep that night? How could she tell if she were in love? She'd never been in it before, didn't know what it felt like, what it was supposed to feel like. She felt dizzy and nervous one minute, dreamy and giddy the next. She felt weak and tongue-tied around him at times. Was that how love felt?

After breakfast, the shrinking food stores were packed, the horses mounted.

"Let's go, Johnny-Jump-Up!" Hero said, kicking her horse with her heels.

Edith seethed. Until she'd told him, Sonny hadn't known a Johnny-jump-up from a stinkweed. She doubted Hero knew either, figured Sonny had pointed one out to her on their moonlit walk. Imagining the scene hurt. Somehow Edith had convinced herself Sonny was above falling for a pretty face, especially one on a person he so disliked. Now she wondered whether it was reasonable for her to expect him to prefer plain old Edith over gorgeous

Hero. Was she giving him too much credit?

Hazel led them to a trail that followed the river downstream. Edith felt vindicated, until the trail began to climb, the river's roar to fade.

"This all looks familiar," Jed said. "Ain't we been here before?"

"How can ya tell?" Hero said, her irritation returning. "It all looks the same."

"It's not all the same," Edith said. "These are maples." She pointed at trees with limbs hung heavy with drooping moss. "We haven't seen this many of them before."

"It's jes' trees to me, Dusty," Hero said. "I'm sick to death a' lookin' at 'em."

Edith peeked back at Sonny, knowing his affinity for the forest, hoping to find some support. He rolled his eyes in Hero's direction, which irked Edith. He couldn't have it both ways, she thought. Couldn't walk with Hero in the moonlight then mock her in the morning.

"We can't hear the river *or* the train anymore," Hero said. "What exac'ly are we followin'?"

"The trail," Edith said.

"Which trail?" Hero said. "It's split a million times."

"Hazel knows the way."

She thought of the Westerns she and her mother had seen at the movie houses back home. Her mother loved them. "Horse operas," she called them, or "tumbleweed tragedies." Edith recalled one in particular in which a cowboy slept slouched in his saddle as his mount clopped homeward.

"Pony knows the way," he explained to another cowpoke.

"Hazel knows the way to Sonny's farm?" Hero laughed.

Edith didn't answer, did her best to block out Hero's phony mirth. She'd liked it better when she was sick.

Jed maintained a steady stream of whining.

"What's the use a' havin' horses an' ridin' off into the woods if we're jes' gonna poke along some trail?" he said. "I wanna find us a cougar, or some Injuns."

"Go on ahead," Sonny shot back. "An' happy huntin'."

"Oh, you!" Hero said, giggling.

Hazel shied suddenly, whinnied, stuttered to a stop. An old woman stood on the trail ahead. Edith hadn't seen her approach. It was as if she'd appeared out of thin air.

"Who's that?" the woman snarled.

Her hair was gray and wild, her skin brown and leathery, her long nose knurled, her chin pointed, her fingers spindly. She was bareheaded and wore a dress made of what looked to Edith like woven strips of bark. Her swollen feet bore thick, curving, yellow talons. She held a spear, aimed it at Edith.

"We're runaways from a lumber camp," Sonny said. "We're only children."

Children? Edith thought. Was he trying to appeal to the woman's sympathy? Was he scared?

"Only children!" the woman said with disgust, then spat on the ground.

"We're lost," said Sonny.

"On *those*?" the woman squawked. "Bunk!"

She eyed Hazel, showed no alarm, no bewilderment,

leading Edith to wonder if she might be nearsighted, or mad.

"We're not lost," Edith said. "We're just not sure where we're going."

"Ain't but one place *to* go," the woman said, lowering the spear point, shaking her head violently, spitting once more on the ground. "Got any food?"

"A little," Edith said.

"Yep, yep, yep," the woman said, looking down, her head bobbing. "I got stew on if you want it." She started away, gestured for them to follow.

"That's very kind a' ya, Missus—" Sonny began.

The woman spun back around. "Ain't no 'Missus,' sonny, nor no 'Miss.' Neither am I 'Mister,' for that matter." She cackled.

"What do we call ya then?" Jed said.

"Ain't yer place to call me nuthin'," the woman said. "You want me, look me in the eye an' talk. I'll catch on."

"Ya ain't got a name?" Jed said.

"Ain't had much call fer one. F'ya think of sump'm

ya'd like to call me, sonny, go on ahead an' try 'er out. If I like it, I'll answer."

"F-fair enough," Jed said. "But I ain't Sonny. *He* is." He pointed at his brother.

The woman led them to a small cabin hidden by drooping limbs. It looked to be made of bark and branches. It was windowless.

"Sit here on the porch," the woman said, stepped inside.

They all dismounted, sat tentatively on the cabin's porch, which was made of flat stones fitted together like a jigsaw puzzle.

"I smell meat," Jed whispered to Sonny.

"Smells mighty good," Sonny said.

Perdie leaned into Edith's ear. "D'ya think she's a witch?"

"I don't believe in witches," Edith said.

"Ya b'lieve in horses that grow outta the ground?" Perdie asked.

Edith conceded the point.

The old woman carried out two carved wooden bowls of steaming liquid, wooden spoon handles sticking up out of them. She handed both bowls to Edith.

"You'll hafta share," she said. "Got only the two, which is one more than I ever needed."

The thick stew contained wilted greens, small chunks of what looked like a kind of fish, and chopped root vegetables that Edith couldn't identify. She gave Perdie the spoon first, handed the other bowl to Sonny, who handed it to Hero. The woman sat with them, sharpening a rusted knife against a stone.

"How long ya lived out here?" Perdie asked, stifling a sneeze.

"Don't rightly recollect," the woman said, not looking up from her work.

"Ya live alone?" Perdie asked.

The woman nodded. Once her head started bobbing, it didn't like to stop. "Ain't alone."

"Ya got a husband?" Perdie asked, then lost her battle with the sneeze.

"Gesundheit," the woman said. "I can make ya a tea that'll fix that."

"Bet yer a hermit," Jed said.

"Jed!" hissed Edith.

The woman seemed not to have heard, or cared.

"Give me some of that, Hero, 'fore it's gone," Jed said.

Hero looked to Sonny.

"Aw, let 'er eat, Jed," Sonny said.

Jed sneered at him. For once, Edith felt kinship with the boy.

"Ya seen any cougars 'round here?" Jed asked the woman.

Perdie looked up from her bowl. The woman shrugged.

"Ever shoot one?" Jed said, eyeing an old shotgun leaning against the cabin.

"I don't shoot nuthin'," the woman said. "Got no buckshot. Cougar's no good fer eatin' anyways. Too tough."

"You et one before?" Jed asked, eyes wide.

"Once was enough," the woman said.

"What if they attack?" Jed said. "How d'ya defend yerself?"

"They don't seem much int'rested in me. Small as you are, though, I wouldn't go off berry pickin' by m'self."

"I ain't *small*," Jed said.

"We don't need to fret 'em?" Perdie asked the woman.

"Not less ya wanna. I remember kids likin' to get scairt."

She turned to Edith. "So what y'all gonna do? No food. No gun neither, I 'spect."

Edith shook her head.

"Can ya fish?"

"From a boat," Edith said.

The woman laughed. "Y'all don't need to worry 'bout gettin' eaten. Ya need to worry 'bout *eatin'*!"

"Can you help us?" Edith asked. "Teach us?"

The woman stood, walked over to where Edith sat, held out her hand. Edith, not knowing what else to do, offered hers. The woman took it, inspected it.

"Looks like yer no stranger to work," she said.

"No, ma'am. None of us are."

"That why ya run off?"

164

Edith didn't like the sound of this, didn't like thinking they'd run away merely because the work was hard, felt a bit ashamed. Was it true?

"No," she answered. It wasn't.

"Not a bunch a' bellyachers?" the woman asked.

"Hero bellyaches all the time," Jed said.

Edith was finding herself with an odd ally.

"I ain't working fer *her*," Hero said, pointing her spoon at the woman, glowering at Jed. "Let's jes' get goin'. I want outta these stupid woods."

Edith couldn't believe her gall. Even as she was insulting the woman, she was dipping back into her bowl.

"Do as ya please, dearie," the woman said. "Ya want teachin', I'll give it to ya. I'll feed ya, too. But ya gotta work." She stepped off the porch. "Talk it over 'mongst yerselves." She walked away.

"Thanks fer the meal," Sonny called after her.

"Ya ain't even had none yet, ya sap," Jed said. He grabbed for Hero's bowl, but she moved it out of reach.

"Why were ya so rude to her?" Perdie said. "She fed us, didn't she?"

"She gives me the creeps," Hero said.

"I think she's a breed," Jed said. "Livin' out here like one."

Edith eyed Perdie, saw her tense up.

"What's wrong with being Injun?" Perdie said, so that no one but Edith could hear.

"Not a thing," Edith whispered back; then to Jed, "What's wrong with being Indian?" She knew Perdie believed the rumors that she was one.

"Nuthin'," he said. "I wouldn't mind bein' one. No one to boss ya around. Fish all day long."

"Whether she is or not, she prob'ly knows a lot about these woods," Sonny said. "We could use her help."

"I ain't workin' fer no one ever again," Hero said, scowling.

"How ya gonna live without money?" Perdie said. "How ya gonna eat?"

"I've worked enough fer a lifetime. It's time fer someone else to take care a' me."

"Like who?" Perdie asked.

Edith watched Sonny during all this, relished

seeing him cringe at each word out of Hero's mouth.

"Gimme the dang-blasted bowl, Hero," Jed demanded.

"Not on your life."

Edith kept her eye on Sonny.

"Hero," he said through drawn lips. "Couldn't ya let Jed have jest a little?"

Hero smiled falsely at him. "Of course," she said. "I apologize if I was hoggin' it. I'm jes' completely famished is all. Here, Brother Jed." She handed the bowl to him.

"It's practically empty," he whined.

"No bellyachin' now, *sonny*," Hero said.

"Why didn't she say anything about the horses?" Edith asked.

"Think she's seen 'em before?" Perdie ventured.

"She's a witch," Hero said. "She prob'ly sent 'em to fetch us."

"Why would she do that?" asked Perdie.

"For the same reason as the Smiths do: She needs slaves."

"Maybe she wants to eat us," Jed said. "That's what witches do. Maybe it's kid meat in this here stew."

Hero's color drained.

"I say we stay," Perdie said.

"Me, too," Edith said. "How 'bout you, Sonny?"

"Me?" He looked from Edith to Hero and back.

"Yes, Sonny," Hero said with a lilt in her voice. "What do you think we should do?"

Again he looked back and forth between the girls.

"I say we stay," he said. "Learn to hunt an' fish. We're outta food an' we gotta eat."

"Well, if that's yer decision," Hero said. "I jes' din't think ya'd wanna stay here with a crazy ol' *witch*." She stood up, raised her chin, tossed her ringlets, stomped off.

Edith looked into Perdie's scared eyes, said, "She's not a witch."

The woman put Sonny and Jed to work collecting and chopping wood, Hero mending baskets, Edith and Perdie washing dishes in a freshet behind the cabin. Later she showed Edith and Perdie how to make fish traps from cedar withes, then led them down to a swell in the stream where the water pooled. They threw in the traps; when they pulled them in, one held a flopping red salmon.

"When they're jumpin' ya can 'bout snatch 'em outta the air," the woman said.

She showed them the best places to find berries, which ones were tasty (raspberries, blueberries, huckleberries, salmonberries, salal berries), which delicious (blackberries, saskatoons), which would do in a pinch (bitter soapberries, bland gooseberries, mealy bearberries), which to avoid (poisonous white snowberries and devil's club berries, though both could be made into shampoo). Jed gobbled berries till his stomach ached. The woman made him a foul-smelling tea to soothe it.

"She's got a tea fer ever'thing," Perdie said to Edith. "The one she made fer me pert near licked my sneezin'." She sneezed, then laughed her horsey laugh. "I said pert near!"

The woman pointed out which leaves were edible

(miner's lettuce, cow parsnip before it flowered), which nuts, roots, and bark were. In her opinion, the inner bark of the red alder tasted the best. She showed them the crab apples that were too tart to eat until they were submerged awhile in a cedar box. She told them the name of the peculiar white flower with the white stalk and leaves they had been seeing: It was called a ghost flower. The flower with the red-and-white striped stems was a barber's pole. While she talked, the girls collected.

"Plants are alive, y'know," the woman said. "Same as us. They don't talk like us, thank heaven, but they speak. Ya jes' gotta listen."

Over the next couple days, she taught them how to use pitch for calk, which wood was best for what: hemlock for fishhooks, alder for cups and bowls, fir for spears. Jed collected plenty of fir. The woman showed Edith and Perdie how to make clothing out of bark, helped Edith weave a skirt out of it. She was an impatient teacher—tetchy, Mrs. Keckonius would say—but her energy rarely flagged. She did not behave like anyone her age that Edith had ever met, though Edith was unsure what that age was: eighty? Ninety? The woman skipped over logs, scaled massive stumps, laughed randomly and madly, her head tossed back.

Despite her quick temper, everyone admired her—all but Hero, that is. Hero complained continually about the hard work, about staying so long.

"Who needs to learn how to survive in the woods? Only hermits, Injuns, and witches live in the woods."

Everyone, including Sonny, wearied of her. Edith enjoyed watching Hero's spell on Sonny weaken, enjoyed seeing his love of the woods rekindled. He was the most ardent of the old woman's students. His respect equaled Hero's impudence. It was clear the woman took a shine to him as well. She especially loved his fiddle playing. She asked him to play each night, dancing and cackling to his jigs, reels, and waltzes. Hero, sulking, sat them out.

Sonny stopped talking about getting to his farm, never mentioned his pa. Edith wondered whether the reason was the lure of the woods, the wisdom of the woman, or just plain fear of facing his father after such a long time, of confronting him about his abandonment of the boys and their resentment toward him for it. Before Hero had wormed her way between them, Edith could have asked him. Maybe, she thought, she'd be able to again soon.

Days stretched into weeks. Scarlet blossoms blanketed the horses, attracted swarms of bees, butterflies, and hummingbirds.

"That is the purdiest thing I ever seen," Perdie said.

"Yep," Edith said with a wink. "Real purdy, Perdie."

Jed kept running names by the old woman. She never acknowledged any of them, till one day, when Sonny whispered something into his brother's ear.

"Hey, Hodag!" Jed hollered.

"Who called?" the woman answered, cupping her ear.

"By gum, her name's Hodag!" Jed said, laughing.

"What's 'Hodag'?" Edith asked.

"It's what the loggers call sump'm in the woods

they ain't never seen b'fore," Sonny said. "An' b'lieve me, they think they seen it all."

"She's strange, all right," Hero said under her breath.

"You don't know the half of it, sweetie pie," Hodag said.

Once as they were out collecting bark, Edith slipped and called the woman "Mama." Hodag only smiled, said nothing, but then Jed and Perdie slipped and it soon became a habit.

"Hang it, I ain't yer ma!" she said, after Perdie slipped again one night during supper. "I ain't nobody's ma, nor nobody's child, neither!"

"How can ya be nobody's child?" Jed asked.

"I jest ain't!"

When Hero snickered, the woman turned on her, her crooked finger jabbing at the air. "An' what are you, little Hero? You a child? A woman? A *mama*?"

Hero's face, her shoulders, her whole being collapsed. She turned green, as if she might throw up.

Edith put an arm around her. "You all right?"

"I want . . ." Hero muttered.

"What?" the woman demanded, her eyes ablaze. "What d'ya want, li'l missy?"

Hero stiffened up, shook Edith away.

"I want to be somewhere else!" she said, the bristle back in her voice.

Hodag leaned forward; in a low, malicious voice tinged with satisfaction she said, "There ain't nowhere else, sunshine."

CHAPTER
Nine

The cabin was a single room. On its plank floor lay a woven bark mat. Hodag slept wrapped in an elk skin in a corner on a bed of dried fern fronds. Edith huddled in another corner with Perdie under blankets and slickers. Sonny and Jed took the opposite corner. Hero had slept in the fourth.

She rode off on Johnny after the confrontation with Hodag. Edith and Sonny went after her, hunted for her until dark, Edith conflicted over how much she wanted to find her. They didn't find her. They spent the next day searching as well, and the next, before acknowledging defeat. Hodag did not help, showed no remorse or even much concern.

"She'll find her own way," she said. "Ever'body's gotta."

Edith wondered what it was Hodag had said that had upset Hero so, why the two of them were perpetually at odds. Were they too different or too alike? Why did Hero resent the woman so intensely? Or did she just resent everyone? After all, she'd fled them all, including Sonny. Edith wondered how he was taking it. She didn't doubt that there was something between him and Hero. Was he suffering now that she was gone?

Hero ran off with nothing other than what she had on her back. What's more, she had ignored all of Hodag's lessons. Edith couldn't see how she would be able to get by on her own. As cross and surly as she was, Hero needed people to complain to, boss around, rile, arouse. She needed attention. The only consolation was that Johnny-Jump-Up was with her. Edith hoped that Johnny would look out for Hero, guide her, provide her with company, as Hazel did for Edith.

They continued to help Hodag, but unlike at the camp, they all benefitted from their hard work. The old woman gave them more than a place to sleep and food to eat; she gave them survival skills, gave them knowledge to help them comprehend their surroundings. Edith had never felt so keenly aware of the living things around her, never felt so resourceful or capable. Hodag had shown her how everything she needed was there for her once she knew how to find it, how taking any piece of it—a strip of bark, a berry, a fish—demanded great humility, gratitude, respect. Edith was beginning to see how everything fit together, how everything from a slug to a redwood depended on one another. What's more, Edith came to view herself as a part of it, which was reassuring somehow. She belonged somewhere again. For that she had Hodag to thank.

And yet there was something deeply unsettling about the woman. Edith had so many questions she was not brave enough to ask: Where had she come from? When had she come to the woods? Why? *How?* Had she come alone? Had she always been alone?

And then there was Hodag's reaction to the horses. Edith believed the reason the woman hadn't been shocked at the sight of them was that she'd seen them, or others like them, before. One thing was certain: She understood them. The woman was undoubtedly an equestrienne of some sort. She had good balance, a tight knee grip, good hands; she responded intuitively to the horses' movements. She rode neither Eastern nor Western, but more like the cowboys Edith had seen at the county fair. She even whooped and hollered like them. Edith wondered if this was the reason the horses were skittish around her, which they certainly were. They had been restless ever since coming to Hodag's neck of the woods.

But then Edith and the others were skittish around her, too. The woman's moods turned on a dime. She was generally gruff and irascible, except when she burst into fits of cackling. Her rages could be more frightening than Mother Smith's. At least with Mother Smith, one had a pretty good idea what it was that set her off. Hodag's rages were unpredictable. She had a hair trigger, a screw loose. And she enjoyed goading and taunting them, Hero being a favorite target. Edith got the sense that Hodag had taken pride and pleasure in driving her away.

A full moon peeked through the trees three nights after Hero's departure, telling Edith they had been with Hodag a month. Rain clouds later obscured the moon. In the morning, Edith found a dewy halo of red petals in the mud around Hazel's hooves. One blossom clung to Hazel's forehead, a star of red. The rain had washed away the other horses' blossoms as well. Edith stroked Hazel's forehead, puffed into her nostrils, looked deep into her eyes. They were murkier than usual. The tiny leaves of her moss coat were browning, curling, fading. In one of the petalless flowers, Edith found the same spiny capsules she'd found in her hairbrush that night in her room at Camp Nine. She plucked one out, split it open, and out poured black, furry seeds, lustrous as one of Cathleen's mink coats.

"Goin' to seed," Hodag said, causing Edith to

jump, Hazel to nicker. "The beginnin' of the end."

When Edith turned around, she found the woman grinning, a frosty glint in her eye.

"It's nuthin' personal, dearie," she said. "Ever'thin' that lives's gotta die. Me, you, Hazel, these woods . . . we're all dyin' ever' second, while sump'm else is gettin' ready to be born. Bein' alive's only half of it. Did you know some trees take hunnerts a' years to fall once they die, an' hunnerts more to rot away? Animals move into the snags. Seedlin's grow outta the mulch of the rottin' logs. Death begets life."

Edith draped an arm over Hazel, pressed her face into the horse's neck, wilted into her moss coat. She had never said a word to the woman about her mother, yet she was positive that was what Hodag was talking about. She was saying Edith should accept her mother's death as a good and natural thing. But that Edith could not accept. She would not accept it. It was not natural. It was not good. She took a deep breath. Hazel's scent had changed, become less fragrant, stale.

"Hazel lived fer you," Hodag said. "She was a gift.

She brung ya out here. Now she'll go back to where she come from. To seed. To start over again."

Hazel blasted her nostrils, pranced in place, flicked her ears. Edith clung to her, shut her eyes tight. She felt betrayed by the woman, tricked, as if Hodag had only pretended not to want them around, as if she'd meant on trapping them all along, as Hero had once said. Had she slowly seduced them by teaching them the forest, by putting them under its spell? Had she tried to enchant them?

"I don't want to stay here," she said into Hazel's strong neck.

Hazel took a step, then another, reared up, her front hooves waving. She screamed. When she landed, Edith clutched her mane, pulled herself up onto her back.

"This is where you was sent!" the woman shrieked. "This is where ya belong!"

"Perdie!" Edith called out. "Sonny! Jed!"

She clucked her tongue; Hazel broke into a trot. Edith guided her toward the cabin. The other horses trotted behind.

Sonny, shirtless, stepped out of the cabin scratching his head, his rusty hair standing on end. Jed stumbled out after him, then Perdie.

"What's the ruckus?" Jed croaked, rubbing his eyes.

"Pack up," Edith said. "It's time to go."

Sonny opened his mouth to speak, but Edith cut him off.

"Be quick," she said. "I'm going on ahead." She tapped Hazel with her heels, which set the horse trotting. "Stay away from Hodag!" she yelled over her shoulder. Then she closed her eyes and put her trust in her pony.

"You won't be the last!" Hodag yelled after her. "They's more where you come from!"

As Hazel carried her away down the path, Edith was plagued by dreadful thoughts—of her mother's disappearance, her father's, the loss of Pippin, of Hazel's withering. It felt as though the world offered nothing but pain, bitterness, loss, and death. She belonged nowhere again, had nowhere to go, no one to help her, no one to fill her emptiness and soothe her fear. She hated being in charge of herself, hated her father for abandoning her, hated the cruel sea for stealing her mother away. Hodag was wrong. Death didn't beget life. It destroyed it.

Edith opened her eyes. Hazel had stopped. Ahead, perched on a stump, was the snow-white gull. It hopped, unfolded its wings, tucked its feet into its tail, flapped away, screaming as it soared up into the columns of fir. This time its leaving did not send a chill through Edith, for she chose to believe the gull was sent from her mother to tell her she was doing the right thing. Despite her skepticism about such things, she allowed herself to view the gull's appearance as proof that she was being looked after.

The others soon caught up to her.

"What's goin' on?" Jed demanded. "Why we leavin'?"

"We have to," was all Edith could answer.

"Who says?" Jed said. "I wanna stay! I'm a mountain man now."

"Shut him up," Edith said to Sonny, then spurred Hazel forward.

"Shut up, Jed," Sonny said, and spurred Mossy.

Jed and Champ, Perdie and Princess fell in behind.

The forest was being warmed by golden sunlight streaming in diagonal stripes though the leaves of the canopy. The light played off the thousands of sparkling, silvery droplets left behind by the night's rain. A fine mist rose up from the forest floor, carrying the scent of fir needles. Birds sang. From somewhere, the hush of trickling water filled the air. The forest was a kingdom of enchantment. Edith had no trouble believing that all the magical creatures she had ever read about lived there: Fairies, sprites, pucks, and pixies; trolls, gnomes, hobgoblins, and giants; helpful animals; wicked witches.

Before long the trail became muddy and pebbly. The riders came upon the river, followed it downstream, where it widened. Edith finally stopped, told them what the woman had said about Hazel, how Hodag had wanted them all to stay with her, how she'd said they belonged with her. Jed agreed with the woman, insisted on returning to the cabin. He whined, stomped his feet, threw a fit. Sonny suffered him awhile, then told him to go soak his head. Jed shinnied up a tree, crept out on a branch, snapped off twigs, tossed them into the river, watched them float downstream.

"Hope the horses last at least long enough to get us outta the woods," Sonny said.

"Either way we'll make it out," Edith said.

She looked at Perdie, who was clearly suffering over the prospect of Princess's withering, as Edith was over Hazel's. Perdie did not return the look.

Edith wanted to explain more fully why'd she'd led them away from Hodag, but she wasn't fully sure herself. Had it been Hodag's enthusiasm in breaking the news about the horses, her suggestion that death was a positive thing? The restlessness of the horses around Hodag took on new significance. Edith wondered whether Hazel been trying to tell her something all along: Not to trust Hodag, not to stay in the woods, to keep going. Or had it been Edith's own fears of remaining in the woods, away from people, from home, from riding—*from her father?*—that caused Hazel's anxiety? Did she really still hold out hope of reuniting with him?

She knew how much Sonny admired Hodag, but figured he must also be confused. Surely, deep down, he wanted to get to his father's farm. He had things to think about as well. Edith decided to wait until later to try to talk to him, when they could be alone.

Before setting off again, they ate the little food Sonny and Perdie managed to grab from the cabin. Jed came down from his perch, ate sullenly, scowling at Edith the whole time.

The trail stuck to the river the rest of the morning. The sun burned so hot that Jed and Sonny rode bare-chested. The girls shortened their Mother Hubbards, which were by then tattered and frayed, by tying the skirts into big knots in front of them. By noon, Jed was complaining about his empty stomach. Sonny jumped down from Mossy.

"Let's make us a fish trap," he said.

They all helped collect cedar withes. The trap they made didn't hold a candle to one of Hodag's, but it served its purpose. In less than an hour they'd snagged a salmon. Sonny cleaned it while Edith and Jed built a fire. After it was cooked, Perdie thanked the fish for giving up its life, as Hodag had always done, then they wolfed it down as if there were no tomorrow. Their piggish snorting grew so loud that they all began to giggle. The giggling and snorting led to romping and playful shoving, until at last Jed ended up in the river. Sonny dove in, fished him out. It shook Sonny up a bit—the currents were strong— but Jed just squealed, "Let's do it again!"

The longer they followed the river downstream, the wider and mightier it became. The sun continued to shine; a sweet breeze blew. Edith might have enjoyed herself had it not been for the state of the horses. The moss on all four of them was now browning. Hazel's movements were becoming more and more labored, her limbs stiffer, her body creakier. Now and then there was a loud crack; Hazel would falter, though she never stopped. Similar sounds also came from Mossy, Princess, and Champ.

The night being warm and still, the runaways camped out in the open air along the riverbank. As Edith dreamed of a black whale capsizing the *Petrel*, she was shaken awake by Sonny.

"You okay?" he whispered. "You was moanin'."

Edith tried to focus on him, on the starry sky behind his head, tried to shed the nightmare's grip on her. She'd always been amazed by how convincing dreams could be, confounded by her own mind's desire to horrify.

"Wanna talk?" Sonny whispered.

Edith looked at Perdie, who mouthed the words, "Go on."

Edith and Sonny walked together along the bank, she being sure to keep at least two feet ahead of him. She didn't know why she did this, only that she felt she needed to.

"I know ya think Hero an' me . . ." Sonny began after a while. He flung a pebble into the river. "But nuthin' happened."

This took Edith by surprise. With all that was going on, the subject of the midnight walk he'd taken with Hero had slipped her mind. She remembered how much it had hurt to hear Hero call her horse Johnny-Jump-Up. The thought of it now didn't pain her in the least. Instead it merely shifted her thoughts to Hero, alone in the woods.

"She was flirtin' with me, all right, but we jes' talked about the woods an' flowers an' stuff."

"It doesn't matter," Edith said.

Sonny nodded, started to say something else, didn't.

"I'm not sure why I panicked back there," Edith said, paused, went on. "I just knew we had to go."

She recalled how Hodag had upset Hazel. Horses, she knew, were more sensitive to tension, to danger, than are people. Edith's mother once told her the story of Clever Hans, a horse famous when Cathleen was a girl, that amazed crowds by solving mathematical problems by tapping out the correct answers with his hoof. It was later discovered the horse got every answer wrong if his questioner, and the audience, were hidden from view. A psychologist surmised that as Hans got nearer and nearer to the right number, the people present let on their anticipation in subtle ways—eye movements, muscle tension, fidgeting—ways they were not aware of, but that Hans was. He would stop tapping when he sensed this change in the crowd, which perhaps explained why he was not always exact in his guesses.

"People are not very good at hiding their feelings," Cathleen had explained.

Edith agreed. She always beat her mother at cards. The hairs on Cathleen's arms bristled whenever she held the Old Maid.

"What'd Hodag say t'ya?" Sonny asked.

Edith remembered it perfectly, word for word, but didn't want to repeat it. Anyway, it wouldn't justify what she did.

"It doesn't matter," Sonny said. "I'm glad we left. I'd been wantin' to. Jes' couldn't figure out a way to do it without hurtin' the ol' gal's feelings. I mean, I 'preciate knowin' all she learnt us, but I gotta get to my pa's 'fore he changes his mind."

Edith sighed her relief. "I wish I could say what it was. There was something about her . . . something . . . I don't know . . . *spooky*. Now, don't laugh. It's like Jed said: Maybe she really is a witch. I felt as if she'd built a trap for us, like she'd caught us."

To her surprise, Sonny didn't laugh or smirk; he just asked, "You believe in witches?"

"I don't know anymore what I believe. She told me

Hazel existed to bring me to her, but I know that's not true."

"How?"

"I don't know. I think maybe she came to help me get away from people who don't care about me, who mistreat me. To get us all away. To set us free."

"Kids can't be free."

"Maybe they can if they live with people who love them."

"I wonder what you'll think a' my pa," Sonny said quietly.

"What's he like?" she asked.

Sonny's brow furrowed. "Ain't set eyes on him since I was little. Can't even remember what he looks like. Wonder if he'll even recognize me."

"He will. Bet you look like him."

"Think so?" Sonny said with a sudden smile.

"You think he'll mind about me and Perdie?" She watched his reaction closely, felt a shiver when he flinched.

"I don't know the guy from Adam. It might be okay."

Edith turned, pretended to look at the moon, hid the waves of dread washing over her.

People are not very good at hiding their feelings.

The horses slept on the ground for the first time, their legs folded under them, their coats the color of sand. They climbed slowly to their feet in the morning, their stems groaning and snapping, their eyes dull and dry.

Edith carried the cook pot to the river, filled it, splashed the water over Hazel's back, which revived her a bit.

"Good, huh?" Edith said.

She went back to the river many times, gave all the horses a good dousing, watched with delight as their leaves perked up. As the horses slogged along the river under the warm sun, their coats soon withered again.

"Why we goin' so slow?" Jed griped.

"Cuz the horses are dyin', ya dumb flunky," Perdie said with rare spite.

Jed said little else the rest of the day.

That night the runaways camped again by the river. Perdie collected berries, leaves, and bark. Jed caught a trout. Edith watered the horses. They ate sitting around the fire. Sonny played a mournful Irish air on his fiddle, which reminded Edith of her father.

"Too sentimental," she said. "How 'bout a jig?"

Sonny obliged her. She and Perdie danced together around the fire, barefoot, holding hands. When the fire dwindled to embers, they all lay down to sleep under the waning moon.

Darkness engulfed the forest, silenced the song-birds, woke the insects and owls. The stars glimmered behind the tree canopy like sequins on a ball gown. Dread gripped Edith's heart: Would the horses wake in the morning? Did magic die?

"Feel like tellin' me a story?" Perdie whispered.

Edith smiled at her. "Sure."

"'Bout yer ma."

"Okay. One story about Cathleen Cade Kelly, pampered pig-iron princess, comin' up."

"Goody," Perdie said, wriggling like a tot.

Edith once more unfolded the story of her mother, this time focusing on how, in her pampered youth, Cathleen always had her every passing fancy satisfied, her every wish granted. If she smiled at a gown or a hat or a pair of shoes or a saddle or a leather-bound book in a shop window, her parents bought it on the spot. Cathleen was spoiled all right, though she was not rotten; she wasn't selfish, or snobbish, or greedy. She simply loved beautiful things was all, couldn't help herself.

She ceased getting them, however, the day she defied her parents and married Billy Kelly, a lowly sailor hardly deserving of a young woman of such refined tastes and breeding, a poor, uncouth boy not fit to shine the boot of a Cade, her father said. Disinherited, Cathleen sailed away with her Billy, became a poor sailor's wife, then a poor sailor herself, then a poor mother, poor fisherman's wife, poor piano teacher, poor waitress, a poor woman on a budget. She never complained. No longer able to purchase the objects of her desire, she devised other ways of acquiring them. She and her daughter borrowed books from the library, returned them on time to avoid fines. They window-shopped, sometimes waltzed into elite boutiques to try on the latest Paris fashions, all the while hovered over and glared at by suspicious salesladies eyeing their less than glamorous apparel. But Cathleen spoke the language of fashion so fluently, spoke with such charm and wit, that she inevitably won the salesladies over. Often she was asked if she wouldn't consider becoming a saleslady herself. Each time she demurred. She didn't want to fawn over snooty old women with bejeweled lapdogs, she told Edith.

"Women like my mother!" She laughed in that country-club laugh of hers.

Cathleen's lone indulgence were the horses, Pippin and Emma. To pay their stabling fees she abstained from all fripperies, even hats. (She adored hats.) Pippin and Emma lived in the lap of luxury, even if their benefactors couldn't. Edith and her mother visited them at the stables at least once a day. Cathleen in her riding habit, Cathleen and Emma at a canter, Cathleen more at ease astride a horse than most people were on a chair: These were the things her heartsick daughter could not forget long after the tragic day the ferry carrying her mother home from the specialist sank in the harbor, the day she disappeared for good.

"She drown'ded, huh?" Perdie said.

"So they say," Edith said.

The next morning they set off again, the horses more enfeebled, yet just as tireless. Watering did less to abate their withering than it had the day before. Edith fretted their stability, their sure-footedness on the rocky bank. But on they plodded. By noon the river was feeling imposing to Edith: Too broad, too deep, too strong.

The weeks of riding, working, and sleeping outdoors were catching up to the flunkies. Few words passed between them.

Near dusk, the river bent sharply around a high promontory, revealing a sprawling stump garden on both sides of the river. The sudden sight of the great green forest shorn to stubble stopped the riders short. They stared, stunned, at the devastation.

"Why they gotta chop 'em all down?" Perdie said.

Edith smiled, remembering how Perdie formerly feared the woods.

"Look," Jed said, pointing. "Smoke!"

A black cloud of it hung over the horizon.

"Must be a camp," Edith said.

"How do we get across?" Jed asked.

"There must be a bridge," Sonny said.

Unbidden, Hazel took a step toward the river's edge.

"Whoa, girl," Edith said.

Hazel didn't stop.

Edith tugged on her mane. "Whoa, Hazel!"

The horse continued on, waded into the rushing water. The river lifted her, with Edith on her back, carried her downstream like a log. Edith grappled with Hazel's mane, which was now slick as seaweed, gave up, dug her fingers through the horse's moss coat, closed them around the wooden skeleton within. The cold river water soaked her feet and legs, sloshed over her lap. She pressed her knees firmly against Hazel's belly, hooked her toes into her web of branches. Edith could feel Hazel's feet pawing the water, paddling, keeping herself upright. She looked over her shoulder, saw the other three horses with their three riders floating downstream. Jed was whooping it up, having the time of his life. Not so Perdie. She was clinging to Princess's neck as if it were a mast in a gale.

The horses picked up speed as they coursed down the river, turning when it turned. The banks whisked by, flattened, spread. The current quickened.

"Faster'n the trail!" Sonny said.

Edith twisted around, found she was able to smile.

"Yee-haw!" Jed yelled, waving his cap in the air.

After a time even Perdie seemed less petrified.

Edith recalled the time she and her father had tried river canoeing, how he had thoroughly disliked having to go in one direction instead of any, as he could at sea; how he disparaged it as "sport"—one thing, he said, sailing was not, should never be.

"Sailing's a way of life," he told her. "Sport's a diversion."

"But it's fun," Edith replied.

As was riding Hazel down the river.

The river twisted again, and Edith and Hazel plunged over a small cascade, sank deep into white water, resurfaced, Edith still on the horse's back, soaked to the skin, coughing and sputtering. When she peeked back she saw Sonny and Perdie, still aboard, also drenched. Champ, however, was riderless.

"JED!" Edith screamed.

Sonny pointed, yelled, "He's here!"

Sonny and Mossy trailed close behind Champ, yet could do nothing to catch up to him. Perdie and Princess were ahead, but Edith knew Perdie couldn't help.

"Whoa!" Edith said, pulling back on Hazel's mane. Hazel stopped paddling, turned slightly, fought the current. Champ gained on her.

"Hold on!" she yelled.

When at last Champ caught up, Edith found Jed in the water, clinging to his horse's tail. Edith leaned over, grabbed Champ's mane, pulled him toward her, let him ease ahead. She grappled for Jed's suspenders, caught one. The boy's weight nearly dragged her off her horse. Holding on to Jed slowed Hazel's progress enough for Sonny to catch up, to help Edith heave Jed, in his sopping dungarees, back up onto his horse. He threw his arms around Champ's neck, spat up a pint of the river. Edith blew a sigh, glanced at Sonny, who winked at her.

She straightened up, got her bearings, saw that suddenly the smoke from the camp was much nearer, and that up ahead, to starboard, lay a narrow strip of beach.

"There!" she yelled, pointing at it.

Sonny nodded.

The current eddied as they neared the beach, spinning the horses, grounding them. Hazel's hooves struck the river bottom. She struggled out of the river, water draining from her body in streams.

"Attagirl, Hazel," Edith said, patting her neck.

"Why'd we stop?" Jed complained as he and Champ reached the shore. "It was jes' gettin' good!"

"We don't want to be seen," Edith said.

"Why not?"

"Clam up an' think, Jed," Sonny said. He jumped down off Mossy, squeezed water out of his pants.

Perdie, shivering furiously, her teeth clacking, sailed in on Princess. She let Edith help her down.

"Edith!" Sonny yelled. "Look at Hazel!"

Edith turned, saw Hazel's head loll and knees buckle, watched her collapse into the sand. She rushed to her side.

"What is it, girl?" Edith said, though she knew. The excitement of the ride down the river had just distracted her. No amount of water was going to save Hazel now.

"What's in her hoof?" Perdie said.

Edith knelt, found an appendage resembling a parsnip protruding from the bottom of Hazel's foot. It was wriggling, sluglike, alive. Three others like it had issued from her other hooves. All four of them curved downward toward the sand, bore into it.

"Roots?" Sonny said, crouching to look at them.

Edith thought of how the horses never budged

while resting. "That must be how they eat."

"It's helping," Perdie said.

It was true. A bit of luster returned to Hazel's eyes.

A moment later, the appendages withdrew from the sand, disappeared back into the horse's hooves. Hazel clambered uneasily to her feet.

"Whoa!" Edith said.

Hazel began to hobble away. Edith followed, reading Hazel's walking off as a sign she could no longer bear a rider. Edith didn't mount her. The horse found a path leading to the ridge overhead, scaled it. Atop the bluff was the stump garden, beyond it, a logging camp.

When Edith spied the camp she called out to the others. They rode their horses up the ridge. Hazel came to a stop beside an enormous, unearthed stump, its thick, tentacled roots frozen lifelessly against the sky. At the base of the stump was a shrub covered with drying brown moss.

Edith crouched beside it. "It's Johnny-Jump-Up," she said. She looked around. "I wonder where Hero is."

Perdie kneeled beside Edith. Her eyes were wet.

"I'm so sorry. It ain't right you should lose another one." She sniffled. "Life jest ain't fair."

Hazel then crumpled to the ground beside Johnny, her ears drooping. Edith leaned into her neck.

"Don't die," she whispered. "Please."

Hodag's words came back to her: *It's nuthin' personal, dearie. Ever'thin that lives's gotta die.*

CHAPTER
Ten

The runaways huddled together within the circle of wilting horses, shivering in their damp clothes. The sun had dropped behind the trees, the temperature falling along with it. No fire had been built, for fear of sparking the tinderbox that spread about them. Sonny had argued for heading on toward the camp, or at least back to the wind-sheltered beach, but Edith refused to budge, refused to leave Hazel. It was Sonny's idea to circle the horses around them.

"They'll block the wind, at least," he said.

Again the stars glimmered. The shrinking moon rose. Everyone had dropped off to sleep quickly after such an exhausting day, all but Edith, who sat up stroking Hazel's long face, her brittle mane, her stiffening neck. As she did, tiny dried leaves drifted to the ground. Edith rested her head against her horse's shoulder, listened to her low, wheezy breathing.

Then, from the corner of her eye, she saw something move. An animal sauntered out from behind a rotting fir log. Edith held her breath, glanced at Perdie across the circle, asleep beside Sonny, a soft buzzing sound passing her parted lips. The cougar, long and lean with an incongruously small head, padded toward the circle of horses, its big shoulders pumping, its glowing green eyes locked on Edith. It came within twenty feet of her before vanishing behind a stump, its long, fat tail licking at the air. Edith exhaled, laughed. It was a good thing they had all stuck together, she told herself, as Jed and Sonny had told them.

Then she thought of Hero, off alone somewhere.

The hazy dawn found her still keeping watch, her back resting against Hazel, her eyes scoured from a night of sleeplessness and tears. Hours earlier a change had come over Hazel. Her chest no longer rose and fell. She no longer responded to Edith's touch, her coos, her whistles. The others—Mossy, Champ, and Princess—lay dormant as well. Already returning to where they came from, Edith mused. How long would it take for them to decompose? What animals would nest within their skeletons? What plants would take root?

When it rose, the sun coaxed steam from the horses' wet bodies, from the runaways' cold wet clothes. Edith stood up, shook her numb feet, bent her creaky knees, smiled wearily at her sleeping, mud-caked friends entwined in each other for warmth. She sank her hand into her pocket, felt the prickles of the spiny capsule she'd tucked there.

"Death begets life," she said to herself.

Perdie became hysterical upon discovering that

Princess had died. She screamed, howled, pounded herself with her fists, broke down.

"Princess saved my life," she sobbed. "She was my own honest-to-goodness horse. Nobody else's. She *can't* be dead already."

Jed yelled at her to shut up. When she didn't, he kicked a stone at her, stomped away, his fists clenched in knots.

When Edith approached, Perdie swatted at her, fingers curled like claws. "Don't come near me!" she said. "This is all *yer* fault!"

Edith backed off, knew that Perdie needed time to absorb what had happened.

"They ain't nuthin' lives f'rever," Sonny said.

The four flunkies set off on foot toward the logging camp, led by the smoke, the familiar odors of fresh-cut wood, latrines, livestock, the familiar sounds of saws and train whistles. Along the way they heard the crackle of a campfire, passed tattered clothes drying on stumps and snags, came upon tents and lean-tos made of old sheets, blankets, cord, and dead tree limbs. A cluster of men huddled around the fire, some old, some not so old—some younger than Sonny. They puffed on cigarette stubs, their faces streaked black with train smoke and grime, their eyes gazing at nothing.

"Hoboes," Jed whispered. "That's the life. Hoppin' freights. Bummin' around. Goin' places. Seein' things. That's my idea a' livin'."

"They don't look so happy to me," Perdie said.

"'Course not," Jed hissed. "They're only happy when they're ridin' the rails."

"Why don't we ask 'em if they've seen Hero?" Edith said.

"Think it's safe?" Sonny said. "They're pretty desperate lookin'."

Edith cocked an eyebrow. "Seen a mirror lately, friend?"

They stepped out into the open, walked in half-steps toward the fire. None of the men said a word to them, or even looked at them directly, until an old man sitting on a log said, "Good day t'ya. Care fer some beans?"

"Who us?" Jed answered. "But ya don't even know us, mister."

The man grinned out of the side of his tanned, crinkled face. "Know ya well enough, kid. Leastwise, I 'spect you're hungry." He stood, extended an open hand. "Friends call me Pap."

"Friends call me Jed," Jed said, shaking the hand as firmly as he could.

"Have some beans, Jed," Pap said.

"Thank you kindly, sir." He took a tin plate. "Don't mind if I do."

"Man's gotta eat," the man said.

Jed puffed his chest out. "That's the plain truth."

Edith and Sonny passed on the food, figuring they weren't the neediest present. Perdie ate and ate, all the while continuing to give Edith the cold shoulder.

"You seen a girl come through here alone?" Sonny asked. "Fifteen or so, blond, curly hair, dirty as us, but purdy."

Edith's shoulders pinched at the description.

"Bitter as soapberries, too," Jed added.

Edith grinned.

Pap shook his head. "Alone is she? Not smart out here, not for a girl, 'specially one that's purdy."

"This a Jacobs & Williams operation?" Sonny asked.

One of the younger men laughed. "Ain't they all?"

Sonny nodded. "How often does a lokie go out?"

"Next one's at noon," Pap said. "Goin' some-wheres?"

Sonny nodded again.

"They got work there?" a hatchet-faced man piped in.

A mumbling arose among the men.

Sonny shook his head. "Jes' goin' home to my pa."

The men's shoulders slumped. One of them spat tobacco juice into the fire. It sizzled.

"Best place to hop it is jest outta town," Pap said. "Wait under the bridge on the far side. The bulls never cross the bridge." He eyed Perdie shoveling in her beans, shook his head. "Ain't easy to jump a lokie, y'know. Seen morn'n a few go underneath." He whistled, shook his head, pushed his cap up higher on his forehead. "Seen too many things."

"What time is it now?" Edith asked.

Pap laughed, called out, "Any of you bums got the time?"

The men grumbled, jeered.

"Sorry, miss," Pap said. "Hoboes ain't ones fer watches."

Edith walked along the plank causeways of Camp Four. It was more of a town than Camp Nine, had a store, a bank, several saloons, even a movie theater. Edith figured it was the same sort of place, if not the same place, the Camp Nine loggers used to frequent on Saturday nights.

Tucked between two of the saloons was a tiny shop with the word PAWN painted above the door. It was the place Pap had directed her to, in confidence. Edith had left Sonny in charge back in the jungle, saying she'd go into town, poke around, look for Hero, maybe scrape up some food from the garbage cans behind the Chinwhisker Café, as Pap recommended. Sonny protested, said he ought to be the one to go, but Edith convinced him—privately—that they couldn't leave Perdie and Jed in the camp without a man looking after them.

"Appeal to a man's sense of his brute force," Cathleen used to say. "Then do exactly as you please."

Edith watched the pawnshop proprietor eyeing her bark skirt as she walked up. She slapped the hoof-pick down on the counter.

"How much for this?" she said, staring at him, not blinking.

The man was round of body, round of face, with a round bald head and a blunt black beard, which he was intently stroking. He lifted the pick with his chubby fingers, inspected it with a magnifying glass.

"Hm," he said, several times.

Edith could tell he saw the value in it—the silver, the diamond—knew further he'd pretend otherwise, try to cheat her, so she spoke first.

"I won't take less than twenty dollars."

"You must be deranged, little lady," the man said. "I might be able to give ya a couple bucks fer it, if'n I don't decide to turn you over to the bulls instead."

"I didn't steal it," Edith said. "It was my mother's."

Tears came to her eyes; she brushed them away. She'd done the wrestling with herself over what she was doing, what this meant. In the end, she had no alternative. They had to get to the farm, couldn't hobo it there, not with clumsy Jed, not with Perdie. Edith had to sell the pick, but she wasn't going to take less than enough to buy the five one-way train tickets they needed, plus some food, maybe some clothes.

"Seventeen," she said.

The man chuckled, but did not shoo her away. "Three."

"It's silver, mister. You know it and I know it. And that's a diamond. It's foolish, I know—a diamond-studded silver hoof-pick—but that's the kind of woman my mother was." Her eyes misted over again. She blinked, cleared her throat.

"Well, maybe your ma *told* ya this was a diamond, an' maybe she *told* ya this was silver, but I'm telling ya it ain't worth morn'n four bucks, an' I advise ya to take that an' git, 'less ya really want trouble."

Edith said nothing. She just stood there, trying to breathe in and out, wanting to run almost as much as she wanted a fair price.

"Five," the pawnbroker said.

"Skip it." Edith scooped up the pick. "I'll try over at the bank."

"They won't even let ya in the door, ya little fool."

"We'll see about that." She started to turn to leave.

"You'll get arrested is what'll happen."

"Sixteen," Edith said.

She'd learned haggling from her father. Billy Kelly may have been loose with money, but he prided himself on never being had.

The man pursed his lips, squeezed them with his fingers, squinted like he was looking at her through his magnifier. "Fifteen."

"Done," Edith said.

The pawnbroker counted out fifteen worn dollar bills. Edith signed a receipt, said, "Pleasure doin' business with you, sir," skipped out.

The Chinwhisker Café was across the street. In the window Edith saw reflected a grubby, shabby street urchin. Her hair was a fright, worse than usual.

"I need a bath," she said.

"Ain't that the truth," said a man passing behind her.

A dime was the going rate at the bathhouse next door, showers, a nickel. Edith decided she'd stand more of a chance of being allowed in the café if she didn't stink to high heaven. She went in, gave the attendant a nickel, stepped into the muggy dressing room, pulled off her bark skirt, kicked off her shoes. Her Mother Hubbard was so caked with mud it stood up on its own.

Several other women were in the shower room soaping themselves under the steaming spray. Edith ignored their gawking, tiptoed across the slippery wooden floor to a tap, twisted it. Brown water streamed off her body, the mud momentarily clogging the drain. She lathered up with her penny bar of soap, purred with delight, stayed in long enough to watch all the other bathers go, more come, go, long enough for her fingertips to pucker. The attendant appeared, scowling, told her to either cough up another nickel or vamoose. Edith twisted the spigot.

"It's off," she said, water dripping off her. "Now get lost."

Edith hated having to put her dress back on. The

stench was unbearable, worse than a logger's at the end of the week, worse than a polecat's. She held it at arm's length, carried it to the showers, ran it under the spray, wringing brown water out of it out over and over, shutting off the tap just as the attendant stomped back in. Edith flicked the woman a nickel before she could gripe. She wrung the dress out, pulled it on. It was cold and clammy. When she left the bathhouse, she left the bark skirt behind.

Her Mother Hubbard clung uncomfortably to her as she walked along the main street. She spied a sign in the camp store window that read DRESSES $1. Edith considered it a second, then walked on. She passed the café, deciding to wait until she was on her way back from the station to pick up food and clothes.

The train station was at the end of the street. Seated on her bottom on the plank porch outside it, pressing the heels of her hands into her eyes, sat a girl in a grimy, torn Mother Hubbard. Her hair was curly but matted from lack of washing. The girl looked up when Edith approached, but didn't acknowledge her in any way. Her eyes were bloodshot and swollen.

"*Hero!*" Edith gasped. She knelt down.

"Dusty Smith," Hero said, squinting, her lip curled. "The famous cowgirl. Yippy-ki-yay."

"We saw Johnny-Jump-Up," Edith said, setting her hand on Hero's shoulder. To her surprise, Hero didn't shrug it off. "The other horses . . . they died, too."

"Yer smellin' awful good, Sister Edith."

"I had a shower. A hot one. How 'bout you have one, too? I've got money."

"Father Smith's here," Hero said, jerking her thumb over her shoulder at the window above her head. "In there. With a *la-di-da* lady. A slackpuller."

"Not Mother Smith?"

Hero gave a snort. "*Not* Mother Smith. Look fer yerself."

Edith edged up to the window, peered in. Father Smith was sitting on a bench with a young woman wearing a fine new violet dress, satin and silk by the look of it. She wore a violet cloche hat over bobbed black hair and strings of pearls drooped around her neck. Father Smith was petting her gloved hand, whispering in her ear, brushing his lips against her rouged cheek. The woman was looking down at a lace shawl in her lap.

"He bought her that dress," Hero said. "I saw him. Bought it this mornin'. I watched him buy a ticket fer the noon train. One way. Not sure which of 'em's goin', but they ain't goin' together, an' she ain't altogether happy 'bout it, neither. Take a gander at her belly if yer wonderin' why."

Edith looked: The woman's belly, which she was clearly attempting to conceal beneath the shawl, was bulging.

"She ain't fat, if that's what yer thinkin'," Hero said. "She's got herself a bun in the oven, an' I'm contemplatin' goin' in there an' stranglin' the bastard."

Edith fit the pieces together: Hero's defiance of Father Smith at the dinner table; her "horsesickness"; Hodag asking if she was a "mama."

"How far along are you?" she asked.

Hero grinned through her rage. "You ain't half dumb, Dusty. I ain't had my menses in two months."

Edith took her hand, glanced at the station clock: Half past eight.

"Come with me," she said.

She dragged Hero to the bathhouse, stripped her, ducked her under a nozzle, scrubbed her, dried her, washed her dress, wrung it out. From there they went to the camp store, picked out a blue floral-print dress with mother-of-pearl buttons and lace at the collar, and a pair of black patent-leather mules. Hero brightened when she looked at herself in the mirror.

"A little rough fer wear, but not half bad," she said.

"You're gorgeous," Edith said. "Let's get some train tickets."

They walked through the doors of the station as if they did not care one whit who was there to see. Hero paraded back and forth past Father Smith until at last she caught his eye. He looked her up and down admiringly, till he realized who she was.

"Hero!" he said, jumping to his feet.

"In the flesh," she said, pretending not to recognize him.

"What in hell's name are you doin' here?" Father Smith demanded.

"Well, if it ain't Orson Smith!" Hero said, pursing her lips. "Fancy meeting you here! Why, I'm only catchin' a train, same as you, I 'spect. Don't believe I ever met yer lady friend before." She turned a diabolical smile on the woman.

Father Smith's bottom lip covered his top one as the woman gracefully rose to her feet. She was prim and poised, though clearly distraught; Edith detected hints of agony behind her inky eyes. She was slender, though not sickly, her arms thin as cedar withes. Only her belly gave away her condition. Edith did not fancy this woman to be a slackpuller.

"This is Miss Lila Cruz. She's my . . ." Father Smith began, flustered. "My niece."

Miss Cruz's face tightened. "And you are . . . ?" she asked Hero.

"A flunky," Hero said, taking the woman's hand, shaking it roughly. "*His* flunky, as a matter a' fact, or use' ta be. An' I'm in the same fix yer in, sugar lumps." Her eyes flicked down at the woman's belly, then back up. "Orson's been a busy little fella, seems." She smiled falsely at him.

"Such impertinence!" Father Smith said, trying to muster a measure of authority. "How dare you speak to me in that manner, Hero? Miss Cruz, I assure you this girl is a liar of the first order. I rescued her from a life of poverty, gave her a home, a family, security, but she was beyond help. Coarse, unscrupulous, no good, just like her mother. A floozy."

Hero slapped him hard across the face, then shoved him. He tumbled backward onto the bench. Hero started to lunge at him, but Edith held her back.

"We have a train to catch," Edith said, then looked at Father Smith. "And we don't expect any interference from you, Mr. Smith, unless you'd like us to have a little chat with *Mrs.* Smith."

Hero let out a loud laugh. "Take 'im for all he's worth, Miss Cruz. That's my advice. An' he's worth plenty, even these days. In gold, 'course. As a man he ain't worth the time it takes to spit on 'im." She spat on him.

A crowd had begun to gather.

"That's enough, Hero," Edith said. "It's time to go."

Hero straightened up, smoothed her dress, her hair. She swallowed hard, wiped her wet face with her arm.

"Yes, it is," she said. She spun dramatically on her heel, marched away.

Edith caught up to Hero outside, leaning against a post, clawing at her hair. Edith gently took her wrists, held them still.

"I know you're mad at yourself," she said. "But this isn't your fault. It's his. Hate him if you need to, but don't hate yourself."

The words came out of her mouth, the same words she'd been saying to herself all these months, the months since that night, at home, with her father.

After Billy had broken his long silence by saying Cathleen hadn't been seeing the specialist for her shoulder, that something was wrong with her blood, he buried his face in his chapped, scarred fisherman's hands, kept them there a long time. Edith spent the minutes watching those hands, big like hers, but proportionate on a man her father's size. She wished his hands would take hers, wished he would take her in his arms, hold her.

When at last he spoke again, he did so into his palms, haltingly. "I want ya . . . ta love me . . . like . . . like she did . . . like Cathy did." He did not look up. If anything, he burrowed in deeper.

Edith had always adored her father. When she was younger, sillier, she swore a private oath on the family Bible never to marry, never even to love another man. Her love for her father was that pure, that blind.

"I love you, Pop," she replied.

He lowered his hands. His fingertips settled silently on the table. He looked at her, his eyes blurry in the candlelight, his red-whiskered face gaunt, stony. He had never looked at her like that before. It scared her. He slid a hand toward hers, stroked it along the bones, over the knuckles, down her fingers, grazing lightly with his long, dirty nails.

"I love you, Pop," she said again, her voice quivering. She did not know what else to say. "I do."

He stood slowly, dragged his chair closer. The legs screeched on the floorboards. He leaned toward her, his face sweating, tearstained, his mouth open, his breath whiskey-stained. He leaned forward for a kiss, not the right kind, a new kind, the wrong kind. Edith pulled away, tumbled out of her chair onto the floor. He jumped up. His chair clattered on the floor.

"*Cathy!*" he said—like a madman, Edith thought.

She screamed, scrambled across the floor to the door, ran to the stable, to Pippin, led her onto the street, climbed aboard, hugged her neck.

"Giddyup!"

Pippin's hooves clopped away over the cobblestones.

Edith stayed out all night, dozed in fits on Pippin's back in a shantytown, where everyone stared and whispered—*A horse in the jungle!*—but no one said a word to her. Pippin's big eyes, glowing like a cat's, like the cougar's, watched over her. When it was light, a woman brought her bread. A little girl brought Pippin a carrot.

"Can I feed her, miss?" she asked.

Edith nodded, smiled.

Later she rode home, tiptoed into the stable, thanked Pippin, fed both horses, groomed them, would not let herself look at the house. When finally she relented, she saw her father through her parents' bedroom window—now her father's bedroom—packing things into his tall sailor's duffel. She watched him empty his drawers, his closet, watched him pull the drawstring, sling the bag over his shoulder, leave the room. Cowering between the horses, peering over Pippin's back, she watched her father step outside. His face showed he had slept little as well, that he hadn't corked the whiskey bottle. On his head was his captain's hat, at the usual rakish angle. He saw her, looked right at her, into her eyes, acted as if he hadn't, turned away, walked along the path toward the gate, passed beneath the hazel tree, didn't duck under the low-hanging branch he always ducked. It knocked his hat off. He bent, picked it up, put it back on, adjusted the angle, peeked back at her, turned red in the face, went on, out the gate, away.

Later, Edith broke off the branch and planted it in the yard.

She was fairly sure her father never knew what became of her, was fairly confident he'd sailed away aboard the *Stormy Petrel*, where nothing attached itself to him, nothing clung, where he could come and go as he pleased, a sailor adrift once again, at last, on the seven seas.

"It's not your fault," she said to Hero. "You're just a girl. He's a man. He should've known better."

Hero wilted, slid down the post to the ground. "Bastard!" she said. "Spreadin' his seed around like a goddam hoosier! Fillin' the world up with more Smith bastards!"

"Stand up, Hero," Edith said. "Don't let him see you like this. Pick yourself up."

Hero, blue eyes burning red, shook the tears from her face. She grasped the post, pulled herself up, brushed the dust off her new dress with her palms, combed her fingers through her hair.

"I ain't a girl no more, Dusty," she said. "An' he sure as hell ain't no man."

CHAPTER
Eleven

When Edith and Hero returned to the jungle, they found Sonny, Jed, Perdie, and a few of the men sitting around a stump, embroiled in a card game.

"Go fish!" Pap said with a laugh.

"Hell an' dammit!" said Perdie.

"Been teaching her etiquette, Pap?" Edith said.

"Hero!" Perdie said. "Where'd you come from? An' where'd ya get that *dress*?"

"This old rag?" Hero said. "Why, I only wear it when I'm in the jungle."

The men crowded in around her.

"Whew!" Hero said, stepping back, waving her hand in front of her face. "You boys reek worse'n loggers."

Edith elbowed her. The men did their best to laugh it off.

"Did ya hafta bring *her* back?" Jed whined.

"You clean up nice, Sister Hero," Sonny said with a red face.

Edith watched him looking Hero up and down much the way Father Smith had.

"I ain't yer sister," Hero said coquettishly. "Not no more."

Edith plopped the cardboard carton she was carrying onto the stump.

"What's this?" Pap asked.

"Open it and see," Edith said.

In it were a dozen cans of beans, meat, and peas, two loaves of bread, some cheese, and a box of cheap cigars.

"No whiskey?" Pap said.

"I need to talk to you," Edith whispered to Sonny.

"Me?" he said, startled. "Sure."

When they were at a distance from the others, she pulled the train tickets out of her pocket.

"Five of 'em," she said proudly, fanning them out. "As close to your father's farm as the railroad goes."

"But how?" Sonny said.

Edith gave a playful shrug.

"I can't hardly believe it," Sonny said.

Edith detected misgivings in his voice. And he was blinking like mad.

"What's wrong?" she asked.

"Nuthin'."

Edith's chest tightened. "You nervous about seeing your father?"

Shrug.

"Your stepmother?"

"It ain't that."

"Then what?"

Sonny shuffled, kicked at nothing, sighed, put off answering until Edith was set to punch him in the nose, then said, "I jes' don't know what my pa's gonna say."

Again he reminded Edith of her father, shrinking away, knowing full well he was going to do the wrong thing, shirk his responsibilities. She sensed his shame at the thoughts he was having. He had to look off, bury his better self deep inside, where it wouldn't nag at him.

What had she expected from him? He was sixteen, a boy, just a boy. All along she knew that.

"Beware of boys," her mother always said. "They're more childish than men."

Sonny wanted to cut her loose for his own benefit, to increase his chances of gaining his father's acceptance. Maybe his father would have been delighted to take the girls in, give them a home. Maybe he, or his new wife, were kindhearted and generous. Edith would never know.

"Me and the girls will go our own way," she said as evenly as she could. "We don't want to louse things up for you. We'll find Perdie's mother. That's what Perdie really wants anyhow."

Sonny started to protest, but couldn't. His lips moved but no words came out. He gave a slight nod.

It was his way of saying good-bye without having to say it.

Edith held out two of the tickets. "These are for you and Jed. You don't want him falling under a boxcar."

Sonny didn't move, didn't speak. Edith stuffed the two tickets into his hand.

"Train leaves in an hour." She turned and walked off.

Edith had the destinations of the three remaining tickets changed at the station, collected a three-dollar refund for doing so. With this windfall, she sprang for showers for everyone. Jed howled in protest, but Sonny insisted. Afterward they went to the camp store, where Edith told Perdie to pick out whatever she liked. Perdie selected a sturdy sackcloth dress and mules like Hero's. Sonny and Jed bought bib overalls, chambray shirts, socks, and brown leather boots.

"Look at the hoosiers!" Hero taunted.

Edith wouldn't buy clothes for herself.

"I'd rather wait till we find Perdie's mother," she said. "Till we have a place to stay."

"What if we don't find her?" Hero said.

"We'll find her all right," Edith said, glaring at her. She didn't want Perdie to fret. "But it might take time. We might have to rent a room." She didn't want them ending up on the streets, or in a hobo jungle.

"Well, if you ain't gettin' nuthin', neither am I," Perdie said.

"An' I ain't gettin' on a train with ya lookin' the way ya do," Hero said. "Pick yerself out a dress or I'm takin' off mine right here an' puttin' it on ya, an' I don't care how much ya fuss."

Edith gave in, bought a sackcloth dress like Perdie's. She refused to buy new shoes, saying hers still had life in them.

"No kinda life I'd be happy livin'," Hero said.

The cost of the clothes, plus a needle and thread, a box of matches, two wool blankets, some jerky, chewing gum, and a deck of cards exceeded the three dollar windfall, so Edith dipped into the money left over from the selling of the hoof-pick, money she'd intended on saving, just in case. She had to dip into it again after taking everyone to lunch at the Chinwhisker Café, where they had hot roast beef sandwiches, mashed potatoes and gravy, and strawberry pie for dessert, along with glasses of cold milk, cups of coffee for Edith and Sonny, and a lemon-lime soda for Hero. The check came to a little under a dollar. Remembering how hard her mother worked when employed as a waitress, Edith left a quarter tip.

"Big spender," Hero said.

The train was twenty cars long, with a shiny black engine in front, a tender, a few passenger cars, some boxcars, and a chain of skeleton cars loaded down with logs destined for the sawmill. Edith had bought third-class tickets, which meant they'd be riding in an open car with backless wooden benches. Lila Cruz also rode in the third-class car. Father Smith was nowhere to be seen.

"Cheapskate," Hero said under her breath.

She walked over to the woman, said something, sat down beside her, commenced to talking.

The whistle shrieked. The lokie stack blew a

plume of roiling cinders into the air, some of which settled on the third-class passengers. The train lurched. The couplets clanked. Edith, lost in thought, slid across the bench into Sonny. He briskly scooted away, flashed a pinched smile, retreated back into himself.

From the train, the handiwork of the lumber company was plain to see. The mountainsides flickered green, gray, green, gray; forest, clear-cut, forest, clear-cut. Edith wondered how many trainloads of logs left how many camps each day, every day, all spring and summer. How much longer before everything was stumps and kindling?

The skeleton car behind them carried a pyramid of six logs, each a good four feet in diameter. There were hundreds of rings in the saw-cut ends, each ring, as every child was taught, a measure of the tree's life, a calendar of past centuries. How long, Edith wondered, had the trees on the skeleton cars been alive? Had they stood since the American Revolution? The Renaissance? The Middle Ages? What lives will the death of these ancient trees beget? They will be cut into boards, she knew, then assembled into houses, furniture, stables, ships, planes, coffins, or milled into paper for books, magazines, and privies. Only when allowed to rot would the wood return to the soil, the coffins and privy paper first.

Jed hung over the edge, watched the wheels whir, pointed out an elk herd, thrilled when the train crossed the bridge. Edith craned her neck out over the side, watched hoboes leaping into the box-cars.

The train slowed as it neared Sonny and Jed's transfer station two hours later, enabling some of the hoboes to jump off—"join the birds," the loggers said. When the train came to a stop, Sonny was already standing, staring out, away, ahead, impatiently tapping a foot. He didn't wait for word from the conductor, for a step stool to be set on the platform, for the car's gate to be opened. He sprung over it, fiddle case and bindle tucked under his arm, hit the ground running.

"Wait up!" Jed yelled over the gate. His feet slid out from under him as he hit the platform and he fell onto his backside. He quickly scrambled to his feet, chased after his brother.

Sonny stopped, turned his body around, not his feet, yelled, "Hurry up! We gotta catch our train!" He looked in the general vicinity of Edith, waved his hand in the air, looked away. Jed caught up to him and they disappeared into the crowd.

A hand slipped into Edith's.

"Jes' say good riddance to 'im, the ingrate," Hero said. "They all of 'em think they throw two shadows."

"Good riddance, Amnon Persons," Edith said.

"The ingrate."

Miss Cruz disembarked as well. She hugged Hero good-bye. "Write to me," she said.

"I will." Hero looked to Edith. Edith nodded: She'd help.

An hour later the train reached the familiar bay, brilliant blue that day under a rare cloudless sky. Edith, beyond exhausted, beyond feeling, strained to see the city in which she had grown up, yet dreaded the flood of memories it was sure to trigger.

The train whistle startled her. Again, a band of hoboes bailed out early.

"We're here," Edith said, nudging Perdie, asleep in her lap.

Perdie snapped upright, widened her eyes. Her fingertips went to her mouth. She gnawed at them.

Edith had been so lost in her own worries, she'd neglected to register Perdie's. Perdie was expecting to see her mother, who she believed would not only be easy to find, but also cured, sane, and eager to reclaim her brave, long-lost daughter. Edith had grave doubts about any part of this. For one thing, if her mother had recovered and been released from the mental hospital, why hadn't she come for Perdie? Maybe she'd been afraid to. Maybe she didn't want to. If so, it would mean finding her would be difficult. If they did find her, what would be her reaction? Would she reject Perdie, shun her, send her away? If she hadn't been released, wouldn't the hospital contact the authorities about the girls, loose on the streets, homeless? Wouldn't they be sent back to their legal guardians, the Smiths? Edith would not permit that to happen. Under no circumstances would they be going back to Camp Nine.

The train pulled into the station, which was a vast web of tracks. Gulls were everywhere, hanging in the air as if on wires, scrounging the yard and the platforms for food, like bums. Edith had been to the station many times before, the last time being the day she boarded the train for Camp Nine with only a hoof-pick, a hazel branch, and the clothes on her back to show for her life.

"Pa was killed here," Perdie said. "Run over by a lokie. Don't know where exactly." She scanned the tracks vaguely, as if something might mark the awful spot. "It's what pushed Ma over the edge, y'know." She looked at Edith. "Where do we look for her?"

"In the nuthouses," Hero said. "World's gotta be full of 'em."

Edith shot her a look. "We'll find her," she told Perdie. "Don't you worry."

They wandered through the crowded train station, out into the city. Even though Edith had lived there her whole life, she was startled by it, by how starkly it contrasted with the deep woods. There were no places in the city without a trace of mankind, where there were no people, pets, concrete, steel, glass, paint, rubber, fabric, garbage, oil, fumes, machines, noise. The few plants to be found were planted carefully, for shade, for decoration. Wildlife consisted of pigeons and squirrels, which fed mostly on what the humans discarded. Again Edith wondered whether there could ever have been a forest here. It must have required a lot of logging, and logging camps.

People in rags shuffled along the sidewalks, going nowhere, hands out, while men and women in crisp suits and fresh dresses, with briefcases and shopping bags in hand, strode swiftly toward their destinations. Teenagers boarded streetcars in bunches, jostling and nudging each other, snickering at the "bums," the "hoboes," the "vagrants," many of whom were but teenagers themselves, Edith's age, Sonny's. Like the flunkies, they appeared older, more weary and weathered, due to exposure to hard work and the elements. Those who couldn't afford the fare begged for a ride, mumbled bitterly to themselves when the conductor rebuffed them.

More of the city's storefronts were boarded up than when Edith had left, more folks slept on benches, in doorways, on the sidewalk, in the gutter. She peeked at each face going by, both hoping and dreading to find a familiar one, a part of her wanting to reconnect with her past, the other wishing to ward it off.

Hero was conspicuously silent as they walked along. Edith guessed she'd never seen an automobile before, much less a streetcar, or tall buildings, or people dressed in such fine clothes.

"Sure a lotta Q's here," Hero said finally, with a sneer.

Edith glowered at her. She knew "Q" was what the loggers called someone from China, and she knew the word was never said fondly.

"Don't ever say that word again. You want people thinking you're a dumb ape? *I'm* starting to think it."

"What word?" Hero said, feigning innocence.

"You know."

"You like 'Chinks' better?"

Edith looked around, mortified, praying no one heard. She slowed her pace, put some distance between herself and Hero, wondered how she could ever have cared for someone so hateful.

"Will you two stop actin' like babies?" Perdie said. "We're s'posed to be lookin' fer my ma. I'm gonna ask that officer over there fer help."

She ran up to the man in her lopsided way. He gave her directions to a mental hospital nearby.

Edith had imagined a sprawling estate with a high wrought-iron fence, nurses escorting trembling, raving, drooling patients around the grounds, a misconception she'd probably gotten from novels and the movies. In truth, it looked no different than any regular hospital: It was a brick building on a street with other brick buildings.

They asked the clerk at the front desk whether a Birdie Bricker had ever been admitted there. He asked whether Birdie was her legal given name. Perdie didn't know, couldn't remember. He asked them to wait while he checked his records. The girls sat in a row of wooden chairs, opposite a white-haired, smartly-dressed woman wearing a fur stole draped over her shoulders. Her hat was decorated with feathers and dried berries. She peeked at them over her waiting-room magazine.

"Mind yer own yard, ya old bat," Hero said.

The woman dove behind her magazine. Edith didn't much like the name-calling, but had been thinking much the same thing.

No Birdie Bricker had ever been a patient at the hospital, the clerk said when he returned. Nor had she ever been one in the second hospital they checked. They were referred to a third.

"Told ya," Hero said, as they set out for it. "World's full of 'em."

They scaled a steep hill. At the top, Edith stole glances over her shoulder, knowing from there she would be able to see the stables where she and her mother had kept their horses, the paddocks where Edith had learned to ride, learned to fall. Glances were all she could bear.

The third hospital had never admitted a Birdie Bricker, either. The clerk suggested they try the missing persons bureau at the Hall of Records.

"It's just down the hill—" the man began.

"I know where it is," Edith said.

The sun was low as they descended, the harbor placid, host to vessels—sailboats, touring boats, tugs, ferries—poking and chugging along. Edith had often eaten crabs with her father on the wharf, cracking their red skeletons, picking the white meat out with her teeth—like a dog, she'd always thought. They'd kept the *Stormy Petrel* in a slip in the marina in those days.

"I know a quicker way," Edith said, choosing a route minus the view of the bay.

The missing persons bureau did have information about a Birdie Bricker. The clerk said she had died three years before, in a fall. Edith saw the word SUICIDE typed in on the form under the heading CAUSE OF DEATH, was appreciative the clerk (whom she recognized) didn't read the word aloud, was glad for once Perdie couldn't read.

She helped Perdie to a chair, sat beside her. Hero stayed at the counter, flirting with the clerk. Knowing from experience that words did no good, Edith took Perdie's hand in hers, held it tightly. Perdie stared without looking, as if in shock. Her body rocked side to side, like a metronome. She blinked and tears streamed down her cheeks. Her body lurched, shook, writhed, emptied. It was like an attack, a revolt. Edith wrapped her arms around her, fell apart as well. The two of them clung to each other there in the cold, sunless lobby, crying like babies for their mothers.

Hero walked up, stood over them, said, "She offed herself."

Perdie looked up, sniveled, struggled to catch her breath. "Offed h-h-herself?"

Edith held her tighter, scowled at Hero.

"Yeah," Hero said. "Did herself in. Y'know, killed herself."

Spiteful words rushed to Edith's lips, but she suppressed them.

"Killin' yerself's the last resort of cowards," Perdie

said vaguely. "That's what Ma said when Pa did it." She looked at Hero. "Did the man say whuther she was an Injun?"

"You an Injun?" Hero said.

"Will you shut up!" Edith snapped.

"I'm jest askin'!"

"I ain't ashamed to be a blood," Perdie said. "Nuthin' wrong with it, Ma says. Cain't help whatcha are."

"Your ma was a wise woman," Edith said.

"Din't do her a bit a' good," Hero said.

"Sit with her a minute, Hero," Edith said. "I'll be right back."

"What d'ya mean, 'sit with her'?" Hero said.

Edith stood, moved in close to Hero's face. "*Sit* with her, Hero," she said, her teeth clenched. "And be *nice*."

She walked away, toward the counter, didn't look back to see whether Hero did as she had asked.

"My mother disappeared last January," she said quietly to the clerk. "In a ferry accident. I'd like to know whether she was ever found."

"What's your mother's name?" the clerk asked. Edith felt sure he recognized her.

"Cathleen Cade Kelly."

He looked into her eyes, nodded, walked away.

While he was gone, Edith focused on the big clock on the wall, watched its second hand sweep, tried not to think of anything else, failed. Maybe she's alive, she thought. Breathing, laughing, looking high and low for me . . .

The clerk returned. Edith didn't wait for him to speak, could tell from his face, said, "Thank you," and hurried away.

Edith secretly commemorated her mother's passing by taking everybody to Whitey's Diner, where Cathleen formerly waited tables. A sign in the window read HELP WANTED.

"We oughta carry a sign like that around," Hero said.

They sat at the counter, ate like queens: Corned beef and cabbage, candied yams, pineapple cream pie. The world outside, where they had no home, no family, little money, could wait. They grew giddy, laughed like hyenas at the slightest thing, at everything.

"Knock, knock," Edith said.

"Who's there?" Perdie answered.

"Dwayne."

"Dwayne who?"

"Dwayne the tub—I'm dwowning!"

Perdie laughed so hard she fell off her stool.

When the waitress asked them to quiet down, they stuck out their tongues. They laughed harder still when the grim-looking manager arrived at the table. Edith paid the check, left a big tip.

The sun was setting when they stumbled out the door. Hero wanted to walk along the waterfront, wanted to wink at sailors. Edith didn't argue. She'd decided she had to know whether the *Petrel* was there. More than likely it was on the other side of the world, but if by chance it wasn't, maybe her father could help. She bolstered her nerve, led them toward the marina.

"Where'll we sleep tonight?" Perdie asked.

"We could try a mission," Edith said. "They feed you and give you a bed for the night if you sit through a sermon."

"Can't be worse'n listenin' to Father Grimes," Hero said.

"Why can't we go back to the woods an' find Hodag?" Perdie asked. "We was fine there. We din't need money er nuthin'."

"You go on ahead back, Perdie," Hero said, squinting at a group of sailors ahead, her hips beginning to slink. "I'm stayin' here."

"Don't you have enough trouble?" Edith asked.

"I gotta find a man 'fore I start showin'."

"That's unscrupulous."

"Don't throw no two-dollar words at me, Edith Smith. I can't be no mama, not by m'self, not at sixteen. I ain't got nuthin'. Somebody'll take my baby away from me an' send it off to folks like the Smiths. Ya want that?"

"You think some sailor's going to come along and marry you and solve all your problems?"

"Why not? I'm purdy."

"Yeah, you're purdy," Edith said. "Purdy naive."

"I told ya to clam up with that hoity-toity stuff!"

"Edith, do *you* wanna go back to the cabin?" Perdie asked hopefully.

"No," Edith said as gently as she could.

Perdie pouted. "Why not?"

"I don't belong out there."

"Where do you belong, then?"

"Yeah, Miss Hoity," Hero said. "Where *do* you belong?"

Edith ignored her, looked into Perdie's eyes. "I don't know. With you, I guess, and this ornery Hero person."

"We'd all be together at the cabin, too," Perdie said.

"No dice, Perdie," Hero said. "I ain't never goin' back to that crazy ol' witch."

"Tomorrow we'll look for jobs," Edith said.

Hero groaned.

"Can't be worse than Camp Nine," Edith said.

"I'm findin' me a sailor to do the work," Hero said. "Then I'll just stay home an' play mommy."

"Maybe we have enough for a room somewhere," Edith said.

"But we're kids," Perdie said. "Who's gonna rent to us?"

"I ain't no kid," Hero said.

"We'll just have to keep the fact we're runaway orphans to ourselves, Perdie," Edith said. "My guess is, these days, if you've got the money, there'll be no questions asked."

"Maybe me an' my captain'll jes' sail away an' see the world," Hero said. "Sail away an' never come back."

It was the same fancy as Edith's parents had had, and hearing it made Edith ache.

"I was conceived at sea," she said.

"Yeah?" Hero said.

"It made my mother wish for solid ground under her feet."

"Not me. I'm sick to death a' solid ground."

Up ahead, the sailors piled into a cab, sped off.

"Aw, now *see*," Hero said. "They got away."

"Lookit," Perdie said, pointing at a child walking between his parents, licking an ice-cream cone.

"Want one?" Edith said.

"You bet!"

Edith found an ice-cream stand, bought a cone for Perdie, then went ahead and splurged on one for Hero and herself. Hero had never tasted ice cream before. It was tasty enough to keep her mind off sailors awhile. The three of them skipped along the waterfront, licking and giggling, the masts of the ships swaying overhead against the orange sky. When they happened by the dock where the *Stormy Petrel* had been moored, Edith stopped dead in her tracks. Her arm went limp. The scoop of pistachio rolled off her cone and plopped among the bird droppings on the dock.

"Aw, that's a cryin' shame," Perdie said. "You gotta be more careful, Edith."

"What's the matter?" Hero asked.

"That boat," Edith said, pointing. "It . . . it belongs . . . to an old friend."

"A sailor?" Hero said. "Well, let's drop in on him!"

Edith didn't hear, wasn't listening, stared at the ketch in its slip, at the *Petrel*, looked for her captain, not sure whether she wanted to see him or not.

"I promise I'll be good," Hero said.

Edith walked away from the girls, said, "Stay here," over her shoulder.

"You're gettin' a bit comfortable handin' out orders, Dusty!" Hero called after her.

Edith put one leaden foot in front of the other, like a sleepwalker. She wanted to see him; she didn't. She had to; she couldn't. The *Petrel* was gently rocking, water lapping at her hull. Edith was struck by the varnished masts, the booms, the planks of the painted decks, the hull. The ship was almost entirely wooden, hewn from trees, trees cut by loggers. She'd never been so aware of it before.

A light was on in the cabin. All Edith had to do was call out "Ahoy, Cap'n Kelly!" as she'd done thousands of times before. "Ahoy, landlubber!" he'd reply. And she'd climb aboard. Thousands of times had they set sail, had Edith leaned out over the bow, gripping a cleat, scouring the sea for whales or sharks or, when she was younger, mermaids.

She eyed the mizzen, the mainsail, the jib. Her brow wrinkled. They had not been wrapped by the Billy Kelly she knew. They were tighter, neater. The clove hitch had definitely not been tied by her father.

"What are you *doin'*?" Hero yelled down the dock.

Edith glared back at her, gestured for her to be quiet. When her eyes fell again on her father's boat, a woman was standing on deck.

CHAPTER
Twelve

Edith guessed the woman was Chinese. She had slight shoulders like a girl's, slivers for arms, straight black hair cut in a bob, a tiny nose, wide-set narrow eyes. She wore deck shoes, loose canvas pants, a sleeveless blouse, held a steaming mug in her small, tanned, callused hand. She was a sailor.

"Hello," the woman said—apprehensively, thought Edith. "Can I help you with something?"

"Is this your vessel, ma'am?" Edith asked.

"It is."

Edith's heart sank. She would not be confronting him after all, wouldn't be seeing him again.

"You're Edith, aren't you?" the woman said.

Edith staggered, braced herself against a post with the single ounce of strength she had left.

"Your hands," the woman said. She bounded over the rail, landed soundlessly on the dock. She was a full head shorter than Edith. "They're so like your father's. Your hair, too. Not the color, of course." She smiled. Her voiced softened. "I'm Sugi.

"I'm Billy's wife, Edith," the woman said. She rested her fingertips on Edith's arm, added, "He's below."

Edith folded like a rag doll; the woman caught her by the wrist, ducked her head under Edith's arm: The drunken sailor hold.

"We're comin', Edith!" Perdie yelled from down the dock.

Edith snapped awake. "No! Stay there! *Stay there!*"

She didn't know what was going to happen, but knew she wanted to face it alone. This was about her and her father, and, apparently, this new Mrs. Kelly.

"Friends of yours?" Sugi asked.

Edith gave a little nod.

"They're welcome here."

Edith shook her head.

"Billy said you'd been adopted," Sugi said. "He wanted to find you."

"Wanted?"

The woman's smile faded. "I think he should explain."

Something lit in Edith, burned into something stronger than indignation, closer to rage.

"Yes, he should," she said, climbing aboard her father's ship, the Kellys' ship, *her* ship.

"Wait a minute," Sugi said. "There's something you should know before you see him."

Edith paused, squinted. He's alive, married; he didn't come for her, rescue her from Camp Nine. What more could there be? she thought.

"He was—" Sugi began to say, changed course. "He lost his sight."

Edith absorbed this—lost his sight . . . her father . . . *blind*—determined not to let it weaken her resolve, her outrage. She would confront him on her feet, no matter what had happened to him. There was no denying, though, that the news had knocked the wind out of her.

Sugi climbed aboard, took Edith's hand. "Come inside," she said.

She led her across the deck, each step one Edith had taken countless times at every age of her life. She knew every board. Sailboats, even the biggest, swankiest yachts, are easy to memorize. The creaky three cabin steps were as familiar as her mother's lullabies.

The same deck beams arced over the galley table, one with a carving of a lopsided heart, an arrow piercing it, the words CATHY and BILLY inscribed within. Billy Kelly sat on a bunk at table. Steam from his mug floated up into his red beard. His hair was longer than Edith had ever seen it, well over his collar. A pair of dark glasses lay beside the mug. His eyelids were shut, scarred, sunken. It appeared as if no eyeballs lay behind them.

"Hallo, Dusty."

Edith winced at the familiarity of the voice, the

ghost of a brogue, the rasp, like hers, though less sandpapery.

"I 'eard ya up there," he said. "Yer voice. Yer tread. The surprisin' thing 'bout losin' yer sight is findin' out how good yer other senses are. Always were, I guess." He half smiled. "Ya want me ta put on me glasses?"

Edith said nothing.

"Are ya well, Dusty? Been well-cared fer?"

More nothing.

"Bet you're plenty angry wit' me," he said, and thrummed his big fingers on the table, a longtime nervous habit of his.

"Your wife says you wanted to find me," Edith said. She filled her voice with as much scorn as she could since he wouldn't be able to see it on her face.

"Aye, I've married. Sugi saved me life. An angel a' mercy, she is. An' a' course I wanted ta find ya, Dusty. At least after I came back ta me senses I did."

"Did you lose them?"

"I did indeed. I should'na, I know."

"But you did."

"C'mon now, Dusty. Don't be like that."

"So you were running off. Why'd you come back?"

"A crazy gull . . ."

"A *girl*?"

"Nah, not a *girl*, a *gull*—a seagull. I was up the mast—can't remember why—an' the damn thing swooped down an' . . ." He brought his hands up, covered his face. "It went right fer me eyes, Dusty. Right fer me eyes. I fell all the way to the deck. Broke me leg. It snapped jes' like a stick. Holy Christ, the pain! So there I am, lyin' on the deck, me eyes bleedin', the infernal gull 'oppin' around me, squawkin', me fixin' ta faint, when Sugi jumps aboard. Pity 'er, Dusty, fer what she found! But, bless 'er, too, for 'elping me. She towed me back ta port an' called an ambulance. She looked after me."

Sugi stepped around Edith, sat on the bunk facing Billy, took his hand.

"S'pose I oughta be grateful ta that gull. If it 'adn't attacked me, I'd a' not met Sugi, not 'ad so much time on me back with nuthin' to look at 'cept me memories."

"Why didn't you come home?" Edith asked, her jaw clenched to keep her voice from wavering. "Or send for me?"

Her father sighed, rolled his head back, sighed again. This was the way Billy Kelly prepared to say he was sorry, that he'd been bad. Edith didn't want to hear it.

"He didn't tell me right away," Sugi said.

Edith looked at her, didn't understand.

"I . . ." Billy said to the ceiling, "I didn't know *what* ta do, Dusty."

"He told me his wife—your mother—had died," Sugi said, looking at him with what Edith felt was a mixture of pity and admonishment. "But not that he had a daughter. Or a home. He said he lived on the boat. It wasn't until about two months later, after he had been released from the hospital, that he told me about you. By then you had been sent away."

"I said I wanted ta find ya," Billy said, pleading now, desperate. "Sugi found out where ya'd been sent an' wrote a letter to the family that took ya in, sayin' we'd be comin' for ya when I was able."

Edith seethed, thinking of her father cowering on the boat while she was cowering in the house, thinking of how he could have helped her, how they could have helped each other, thinking what a miserable coward he was. She further seethed, thinking of Mother Smith, how she tried to destroy the letter Sonny's father had sent, how she'd succeeded with the one Sugi had.

"We never 'eard back, thought mebbe the camp 'ad moved on. They told us lumber camps don't stay put long."

"It never moved," Edith said, her words sharpened by spite.

"Now, don't get sore, Dusty. T'ain't easy bein' blind," Billy said. "I 'ad ta learn ta get around. An' I 'ad the damn broken leg on top of it."

Edith saw Sugi's gaze fall to the table, and, in that moment, knew her father had given up. Maybe in his heart he knew what was right, knew he should have moved heaven and earth to find her, knew it was his duty; but with the sea beckoning, he didn't want a daughter around to anchor him. He didn't want his daughter telling his new love what had happened, what had *really* happened the day he walked out. She doubted very much he had told Sugi about it, *all* about it. No, he'd given up looking for her, given up on her.

"When did you marry?" she asked.

"In May," Sugi said. "The eleventh. At City Hall."

"Four months and a day after the ferry sank," Edith said, biting down on the inside of her cheek to keep from crying. "Did you even know for sure she was dead?"

"'Course we did, now, Dusty," Billy said. "Could'na got married otherwise."

Edith didn't know how much more she could take. If this were *Wuthering Heights* she'd have fainted long ago, maybe even died—from heartbreak, from betrayal. It wasn't *Wuthering Heights*, though. It wasn't a story. It was happening. She stiffened her spine, cleared her throat.

"Me and my sisters need a place to stay tonight," she said.

"Sisters?" Billy said.

"That's why I came. We're looking for a place to stay. Not permanently. Just till we get on our feet."

Billy shaped words with his mouth, voiced none.

"We don't have much room," Sugi said. "We sold the house and have been living here on the boat. It will be a little cramped, but you're welcome, all of you, to stay with us."

"But, Dusty," Billy said, "who are these 'sisters'?"

"Their names are Perdie and Hero," Edith said, as if that were all he needed to know. "They're waiting on the dock."

"Hero?" Billy said.

"That's her name."

"But ya don't *have* sisters, Dusty."

"I do now."

"Go and ask them to come in," Sugi said.

"But—" Billy said.

"No buts, Billy," Sugi interrupted. "Not anymore."

Edith started up the stairs, stopped, turned back around.

"Pop," she said. "Put on your glasses."

She went up on deck, breathed in the night air,

breathed it out, leaned back against the mast, marked her height with the edge of her hand. She'd grown half an inch since the last notch had been cut, on the last day of December.

She jumped down to the dock, waved at the girls, called, "It's okay! Come on!"

They came running.

"Is he gonna help us?" Perdie said, out of breath.

"We can stay with him awhile."

"So where is this kind sailor?" Hero said. "I'd like to show him my gratitude."

"He's inside. And he's married, Hero. He's my father."

"Yer father?" Perdie said, perplexed.

She started to say something else, stopped herself. Edith guessed it had something to do with the generally accepted idea at Camp Nine that she was a full orphan.

"That was a dirty trick, Dusty," Hero said. "But yer ma's dead, ain't she? Who's he married to?"

"I guess she's my stepmother. Her name is Sugi. I just met her for the first time."

"Well, I bet he has loads a' sailor friends," Hero said. "Where's he live?"

"Here on the boat."

Hero scrunched up her face. "Is it big enough fer all of us?"

"There are two bunks in the bow. Perdie and I can double up. It's just temporary, until we can find a place."

"Why don't ya wanna stay with yer pa, Edith?" Perdie asked. "Is it cuzza us?"

"No, Perdie," Edith said. "You have nothing to do with it. It's kind of . . . complicated. Listen, I don't want anybody to be shocked, so I'll tell you now: My father's blind. He can't see."

"A blind sailor?" Hero said.

"What happened to him?" Perdie asked.

"An accident," Edith said, for some reason not wanting to say more. "Not too long ago, either. It's not pretty, so be prepared."

"Like we ain't seen it all before," Hero said.

Edith helped them aboard. Perdie was apprehensive at first, mumbled, "Ain't never been on no boat before," but grinned with delight once on deck. Edith felt sure Hero had never been on a boat before either, felt proud somehow for being the one to make it happen.

"Pop," Edith said when they'd climbed down into the cabin, "this is my sister, Hero. Hero, this is Billy Kelly, my father."

Hero looked stricken, not by the specter of Billy's dark glasses, but by the woman seated at the table with him.

Edith saw her staring, added, "And this is Sugi."

Sugi smiled. Hero tried to do the same.

"Such an unusual name you have, Hero," Sugi said. "Very strong."

"Yours is unusual, too," Hero said awkwardly.

"It's Japanese," Sugi said. "It means 'cedar.'"

Japanese, Edith thought, not Chinese.

"Yeah? Mine means 'hero.'"

"Well, welcome aboard, Hero," Billy said.

"Thank you fer lettin' us stay, sir," Hero said, batting her eyelids—for nothing, Edith thought.

"Call me Billy."

"Thank you, Billy," Hero said coyly.

"And this is Perdie," Edith said.

"Hi," said Perdie, looking at the floor.

"Hello, Perdie," Sugi said.

"Does me bein' blind frighten ya, Perdie?" Billy said.

"No, sir," Perdie said. "I seen plen'y worse."

"Both you girls are welcome to stay with us long as ya like," Billy said. "Any friends a' Dusty's are friends a' mine."

Edith enjoyed seeing Hero's jaw fall open, watching her mouth the word 'Dusty.'

Sugi led them to their bunks in the bow. She opened a closet; several dresses hung inside on hangers. On a shelf above them were hats, scarves, and fox stoles, both white and silver. On the floor was a pile of shoes. Edith recognized it all instantly, could see her mother dressed to the nines for a party, her flaxen hair curling out of a cloche hat, her lipsticked lips a bright red cupid's bow, a string of pearls draped down her bare, fine-boned back, her slender arms bangled at the wrists, a sleek chiffon or silk or crepe gown clinging to her wisp of a figure. Cathleen

Cade Kelly was not one to organize her shoes.

"They're your mother's," Sugi said to her. "I insisted we hold on to them should you return."

Did that mean Billy had wanted to get rid of them? Edith wondered. What had he done with the rest of the family's things?

Edith reached in, lifted out a silk gown, lilac, with a buckled sash, held it up in front of her sackcloth dress, pretended to size it, pretended doing so wasn't tearing her to pieces.

"She kept them here in case we sailed somewhere where she'd need to look nice," Edith said.

"Here," Sugi said, opening the closet door wider to reveal the full-length mirror hung inside it.

Edith looked at her raw, weathered face, her grubby nails, her callused hands clutching Cathleen's silken gown. Her mother had owned thirty just as fine, each of which her beauty humbled. Edith couldn't humble them. She handed the gown to Hero, saying, "Purple's not my color."

"Well, here," Sugi said. "Here's a green one. Chartreuse, I think they call it."

Edith passed it on to Perdie, saying, "They're just not me."

At the end of the row of dresses peeked the red wool sleeve of Cathleen's riding coat. Edith lifted it out, found fawn jodhpurs folded over the hanger within, string riding gloves tucked into the pockets.

"This is more like it," she said, holding it up before her.

"There are nightgowns in here," Sugi said, sliding open a drawer. "And there's a curtain for privacy. Billy and I will sleep in the galley on the table bunks. They're quite comfortable. Tomorrow, if you like, I can ask at the restaurant where I work if they need any help. It would probably be washing dishes, though."

"That'd be great," Edith said.

"Yeah, washin' dishes is one thing I'm good at," Perdie said.

"I am certain you're good at a great many things, Perdie," Sugi said, lightly touching her shoulder. "Now, you must all be very tired. I'll leave you to get ready for bed. May I get you some tea?"

"Tea?" Hero said, wrinkling her nose.

"Sure!" said Perdie.

"I'll bring some," Sugi said. She left them, drawing the curtain behind her.

Edith got out two of Cathleen's nightgowns and a pair of pajamas. She handed the nighties to Hero and Perdie. She preferred pj's.

"Sugi's nice," Perdie whispered.

"Fer a—" Hero began, registered Edith's warning glare, didn't finish. "Think yer pa knew when he married her? He was blind, y'know."

"Then what diff'rence does it make?" Perdie asked.

They slipped into their bedclothes, then crawled into their bunks. Edith showed Hero how to put the bunk board in place so she wouldn't roll out during the night. Hero whined that the bed was too narrow, too short. Edith and Perdie lay crosswise in theirs. Sugi brought them tea; they thanked her, bade her good night. When they'd finished the tea, they blew out the lamp.

A few minutes later, Perdie whispered, "Edith, my head hurts."

"I'm gonna *puke!*" Hero said.

"It's seasickness," Edith said, removing the bunk board, climbing out of the bed. She pulled on the riding jacket, collected shawls and stoles for the others. "Grab your blankets and follow me."

Billy and Sugi were still at the table, a bottle of whiskey and a tumbler before them, when the girls emerged. Sugi was mopping Billy's wet face with a handkerchief.

"We're going to sleep on deck," Edith said. "At least till these two get their sea legs."

Sugi gave a knowing nod. Billy hid his face with his hands.

The sun had set. The stars were brilliant in a clear, indigo sky. Edith was struck in a new way by the darkened stretch of snowcapped mountains far across the bay. They had been there her whole life. Now she knew them.

The girls spread out their bedding on the deck, lay on their backs, looking up.

Hero took long, deep breaths, sighed, "That's better."

"You'll get used to it," Edith said. "It just takes time."

They huddled closer together as the night air chilled. Perdie and Hero soon drifted off to sleep. Edith was more exhausted than she ever remembered being in her life, but her thoughts kept her awake. She considered whether to return to the morgue in the morning to find out where her mother's body was, to find out how sick she had been before she died. She wondered about the possibility of tracking down Pippin and Emma, of finding a way to get them back. She thought about looking up Lo (how surprised she'd be!). She thought about her father, the gull, how lucky that Sugi had sailed by that day, what her father had said—and done—that last night at home, and about the hazel branch, Camp Nine, the Smiths, Lila Cruz, Sonny, Birdie Bricker, Hodag, the horses, Hazel. . . .

It was useless trying to sleep. She eased away from the others, tiptoed across the deck, down the creaky cabin steps, found her father sitting at the table in the dark, his face bathed in blue moonlight shining through a porthole. Sugi was asleep, her head on his lap.

"Dusty?" he whispered.

"Yeah, Pop. It's me. What are you doing sitting in the dark?"

He breathed a laugh, cocked his head. Edith understood her error.

"Dusty . . ." he began, his voice soft and frail.

"It's okay, Pop."

"It ain't okay." He leaned forward. "I'm awful sorry, Dusty. Really. I'll make it up t'ya."

Edith didn't answer, couldn't answer. She nodded, then realized she'd made the same mistake as before.

"Dusty? Ya still there?"

"I just came down to get something, Pop." She turned, dashed to the bunk room, fumbled for her sackcloth dress, dug into the front left pocket, checked to see if the seeds were still there.

They were.

She walked back past her father toward the steps. He said something, but she didn't listen. She didn't want words from him, apologies, vows. She climbed the steps, crossed the deck, crawled back in with her sleeping sisters under the stars, wriggled until she was warm again. She lay on her back and counted stars, as she had done as a child when unable to sleep at sea. Her mind quieted. Her eyelids drooped.

Suddenly, she was awakened by the scream of a white gull perched above her on the boom. It was the same gull, her mother's emissary, what Edith had come to view as her very own guardian gull. It unfolded its wings, dived, leveled off, swooped over Edith and the sleeping girls, snapped its wings, sailed off over the waves, over the dark waters that had swallowed up Cathleen Cade Kelly, and countless others through the years. Edith was not the only one to have lost somebody, she realized, not the first even to have lost a mother; she was not the only one in the world to grieve. Thinking that gave her some small comfort.

She stared with aching eyes at the distant silhouette of the forested mountains, fingered the capsules in her hand, felt their tiny spines pricking her skin. She pried one open. Furry, black seeds poured out. Hazel was in them, as Cathleen was in Edith.

"Death begets life," she said to herself.

She tucked the seeds into the breast pocket of her pajamas, imagining a day when she and her sisters might need them.